# JUST CALL

# ME

# SOURCE

## JAMES

## PEIFER

# DEDICATION

Dedicated to Judith Jankiewicz,
aka "Peaches"

# PROLOGUE

The Global balance of power had been significantly changed, due to the de-nuclearization of weapons of mass destruction of the most powerful countries in the world. Many of the countries that had lost their nuclear weapons superiority were in turmoil. Their government leaders were confused, and in fear, with their loss of power and dominance.

China, Russia, North Korea, India, and Pakistan had lost the powerful domestic threat they had used to keep their populations in check, and under control. They had lost their ability to keep their adversaries at a distance. Iran had lost its ability to threaten and dominate middle eastern countries. Iran's pending development of nuclear weapons was no longer going to happen.

The major nations had begun to ramp-up their investments and their manufacturing of conventional weapons. They were beginning to build huge stockpiles to prepare for conventional war.

Even without their advantage in nuclear weapons, the United States continued to have the most advanced, sophisticated, and powerful military in the world. It was the most battle-tested of all nations, since it had been in constant military readiness for over thirty years—ever since the First Gulf War began on January 17, 1991. The United States continued to dominate the world with its economic superiority.

Liberal and Conservative political factions, within the United States, had become hysterical with their bombastic rhetoric. Many warned that the nation was very vulnerable, due to the loss of the nation's strategic advantage with nuclear weapons. Some postured that the United States was now at the mercy of communist nations, whose primary goal was to take down America. At almost every opportunity, Conservatives reminded the American public that, for many years, the Iranians had pledged, "Death to America" and "Death to Israel."

The social media company, Twilight, had been shut down and then revived, after complying with edicts from Jim and the Source to discontinue censoring their users and agreeing to no longer fund political action committees (PACs). Other social media companies "got the message" from Twilight's experience, and they too began behaving more responsibly towards their users. They also refrained from funding PACs, but, in turn, ramped up their lobbying efforts by funding more lobbyists in Washington D.C. to serve their purposes.

The American public remained deeply divided by the differences between the two main political parties. The Republican and Democratic parties continued to grow apart, with the progressive-left moving further towards greater radicalization and the Republican party becoming dominated by the revitalized conservative-wing.

The divisions were reminiscent of pre-Revolutionary War America.

Almost everyone was choosing sides or had a family member on the other side—often vitriolic—tearing families apart.

The Heritage Foundation reported that the rise in violent crime had become a national trend in the past few years. Cities reached homicide rates not seen in decades.

FBI statistics showed a 30% increase in violent crime in 2020 compared to the previous year. It was the largest single-year increase since the agency began tracking those numbers in the 1960s.

After the death of George Floyd in May 2020, while in police custody in Minneapolis, the surge in violent crime began nationwide. The event gave the radical left and communist organizations, like Black Lives Matter and Antifa, the impetus to pursue unrestrained violence and destruction in America. They were encouraged and supported by the leaders of the Democratic Party, left-wing politicians, and the large financial donations from some Silicon Valley companies.

Black Lives Matter founders came under federal investigation and were accused of misappropriation of funds, self-dealing, and tax avoidance. They had taken in upwards of $100 million dollars in donations. Very few of the donations, designated for the Black Community, had reached the people in need. The founders used the donations to purchase homes for themselves and they distributed the money among their family members—as much as $1 million to one family member.

Some of the most prominent cities in America were hit by crime surges and they were not prepared to manage them.

In Minneapolis, criminals burned large areas of the city to the ground and looted businesses. They even burned down and destroyed a police precinct's headquarters. The city defunded and undermanned the police department. Homicides in the city doubled from 2019 to 2020. The city, especially the poor community, paid a high price for defunding and reducing the size of the police force. Many of the poor were required to travel long distances to shop since many local stores, closest to their homes, had been destroyed.

In 2022, Minneapolis was trying to hire more police officers.

Portland, at the same time as Minneapolis, was being destroyed and vandalized by left-wing criminals. Even the mayor, a Democrat, joined the protestors who were destroying the city. He told the media that he was going to defund the police. The protestors eventually turned on him and demonstrated at his home. Portland had over 100 consecutive days of rioting.

Like Minneapolis, Portland had to refund its police department in 2021.

Chicago had some of the largest protests and riots. Its downtown area was vandalized and burned. Chicago mayor, Lori Lightfoot, supported the protestors and defunded the police department in 2021.

In 2022, with rampant violence destroying the city, Lightfoot was pleading with the federal government to intervene and save her city.

Los Angeles, New York City, Philadelphia, and San Francisco experienced violence, crime, and destruction in their inner-cities, due to their permissiveness towards drugs, homeless encampments, and the defunding of their police departments.

New York City withdrew $1 billion from the police budget in 2020.

U.S. Congresswoman, Mary Gay Scanlon, a Democrat from Pennsylvania, was carjacked at gunpoint, in broad daylight, in Philadelphia.

While protests and riots plagued many of the largest cities in America, a more insidious threat was escalating in the nation—**an opioid epidemic.** The United States was experiencing a nationwide public health crisis, and few were paying attention.

As of 2016, more than 289 million prescriptions for opioid drugs per year were written. Legitimate clinical prescriptions of pain relievers were being diverted through an illegitimate market that led to addiction and death.

One in three drug users were prescribed drugs more powerful than morphine. The most common prescribed opioids were oxycodone and hydrocodone.

At this time, an increasing number of opioid overdoses have been related to heroin and illicitly manufactured fentanyl.

In 2019, it was reported by the Drug Enforcement Administration (DEA), that China remained the primary source of fentanyl and fentanyl-related substances being trafficked into the United States. DEA reporting indicated that the Sinaloa and the New Generation Jalisco (Cartel de Jalisco) cartels were the primary trafficking groups responsible for smuggling fentanyl into the United States from Mexico.

The Daily Mail reported that Customs and Border protection had encountered 1.6 million migrants in fiscal 2021. The number was closer to two million, when counting those who had been immediately turned away at the border.

On June 13, 2021, Scott A. Davis of *Law Enforcement Today* reported that the Border Patrol claimed that 250,000 illegal immigrants "got away" into the United States during the first six months. Experts suspected that the actual number was much higher than the Border Patrol's calculations.

"Got-aways" are defined as migrants crossing the border and escaping after being observed by the border patrol either through visual observation of officers, video from aircraft, or physical evidence like footprints on the ground.

**China has become a "Prison Nation."**

Since China joined the World Trade Organization (WTO), in 2001, the Chinese Communist Party (CCP) has imprisoned their domestic population with the world's most complex set of social controls. Using advanced technology, including artificial intelligence, employing tens of thousands of government watchers, and installing over 600 million surveillance cameras throughout the nation, the CCP monitors every aspect of Chinese life. The CCP controls the banking system and reviews every business transaction, both domestic and foreign.

"Our deeds still travel with us from afar/And what we have been
makes us what we are."

~ *Middlemarch* by George Eliot (1819—1880)

# CHAPTER ONE

# WHILE AMERICA SLEEPS

Chinese New Year 2024—Year of the Dragon.

It was 9am on February 10, 2024, and General Secretary Xi Jinping was presiding over an annual meeting of the Standing Committee of the Chinese Communist Party (CCP) in Beijing, China. He sat in the middle of a half-moon shaped table, in a raised chair, and was flanked by three Standing Committee members to his right and three members to his left. The table faced a small audience comprised of staff members of the Committee.

Each subject of the day would be presented, by staff members to the committee members. The committee members would make judgements and policy decisions both during and after the meeting that would be the law of the land.

Even though it was the Chinese New Year that had begun with the new moon, Xi was requiring the Standing Committee to meet while the Chinese people were celebrating their most popular holiday. The new moon occurs sometime between January 21 and February 20—according to western calendars. Festivities last until the following full moon. Since the 1990s, people in China have been granted seven days off work during the Chinese New Year.

Xi Jinping, General Secretary of the CCP chose this date to meet with the CCP's Standing Committee. He was a serious man and was known to push fellow members of the committee to be as hardworking as he was. This was no time for them to be celebrating.

Xi is tall for his generation of Chinese men. He is 71-years-old, born in 1953, and is 5'11" tall. He is married to Peng Liyuan. They have a daughter, Xi Mingze, who was born in 1992. Xi Mingze graduated from Harvard in 2015.

Xi lives modestly, but takes advantage of his high position and power in the government, to enjoy a comfortable life. He is an extremely wealthy man, through entities set up by family members. His mistress is known only to a few of his closest associates.

Xi is divorced from his first wife, Ke Lingling, the daughter of Ke Hua, a former Chinese diplomat. Xi married her because her father was a high official in the Chinese government. He believed that their marriage would enhance his career growth. The two were known to argue "almost every day." They were married for less than four years before divorcing. Xi and Ke divorced due to a "difference in life philosophy."

Ke Lingling wanted Xi to move to England to be closer to her father, who had been the Chinese Ambassador to England. After the divorce, Ke immigrated to England and has been living there since 1982.

Ke Hua retired as ambassador in 1995. On January 1, 2019, Ke Hua died of an illness in Bejing, at the age of 103.

In 1987, Xi married a prominent folk singer, Peng Liyuan. Peng plays a more visible role as the "First Lady" of China, compared to her predecessors.

Xi Jinping is a product of the CCP development program. His father, Xi Zhongxuan, was a comrade-in-arms of Mao Zedong. Xi Zhongxuan was once the Deputy Prime Minister of China, but later fell out of favor after criticizing the government actions during the 1989 Tiananmen Square incident.

Xi Jinping became an official party member in 1974, at the age of twenty-one. By 1995, he had ascended in the Party to the post of Deputy Provincial Party Secretary.

The Standing Committee is made up of 7 members of the CCP headed by Xi. The other six members are Li Qiang, Zhao Leji, Wang Huning, Cal Qi, Ding Xuexiang, and Li Xi. Each of the six have close ties to Xi Jinping and have, in different areas, helped to execute his vision for China's development.

The seven-member group wields near-total authority within China's heavily centralized political system. The group's officially mandated purpose is to conduct policy discussions and make decisions on major issues when the Politburo is not in session. In practice, the Standing Committee is supreme over its parent bodies and determines the direction of China.

The Standing Committee was reviewing the nation's plans for the next twenty years. It is a practice of the Committee to review the next twenty years during the beginning of the New Year.

Staff members of the Standing Committee are tasked with the responsibility to present the global plan in hourly meetings.

The first subject on the agenda was to review the condition of the rice famine that had struck Asian countries in 2023. China's rice crop had been devastated due to high levels of surface ozone. It was determined that India's rice crop was reduced to a 50% yield due to rampant rice-sheath blight. China and India, each with a population close to 1.5 billion people, have been forced to seek greater rice imports and other foods, throughout the globe, to feed their populations.

**Surface Ozone Pollution** – Surface ozone refers to the ozone found in the troposphere—Earth's lowest atmosphere layer extending about twenty kilometers above sea level. As ozone levels increase in China, this form of pollution threatens to decrease the nation's rice production.

**Rice-Sheath Blight** – is a disease caused by a basidiomycete, that causes major limitations on rice production in India and other countries in Asia. It can decrease the yield up to 50% and reduce its quality. It causes lesions on the rice plant, and can cause pre-and post-emergence seeding blight, banded leaf blight, panicle infection and spotted seed.

Ref: Fleet N Lee – 1983

Chen Chu, a member of the staff of Standing Committee member, Li Qiang, had the task of presenting an overview of the condition of the famine in China and India that had been going on for the last four months.

In the 2021/2022 crop year, about 509.87 million metric tons of rice was consumed worldwide.

The three Asian countries of China, India, and Indonesia consumed 90% of the rice in the world.

China alone consumed 60% of the rice in the world.

Asian people consume approximately 300 lbs. of rice annually.

Americans consume approximately 26 lbs. of rice annually.

Chu began, "Last year's rice yield was at 40% and our reserve inventory is greatly depleted. Yesterday's reports from nine provinces were very alarming, and they have reported that thousands of people are dying from starvation. Many people are staging protests and demonstrations, demanding to receive their rice quota.

"Our scientists have informed us that it will take at least a one year to recover from the famine caused by the ozone pollution."

"Chairman Xi. We've been discussing **'Operation Laowai'** the last few weeks. It is time to launch our operation against India and Taiwan. It will focus the people on our adversaries and away from our economic disaster," said Qiang.

**Laowai is Chinese slang for "foreigner."**

"Are you sure this is the right time? We must build consensus in the Politburo for an operation this bold," said Xi.

Other Standing Committee members voiced the same sentiments. "It is time, Chairman Xi. We should not wait any longer," said Leji.

Huning, Qi, Xuexiang, and Li Xi nodded their heads in approval.

"With your consensus, you must notify our military commanders to move Operation Laowai forward immediately," ordered Xi.

Operation Laowai was a plan, developed by the Standing Committee, to declare war and attack India and Taiwan simultaneously. The purpose of the attacks was to divert attention away from China's severe economic conditions, and agricultural failures, that had created famine in many of China's provinces. They believed that the attacks would unite the nation to fight foreign aggression. The Chinese government had used this ploy many times in history to take away any threat to its power.

The Standing Committee had formulated this plan after all nations, possessing nuclear weapons, had lost their nuclear capability due to the attacks from Jim and the Source. At that time, Jim announced that he and the Source would not get involved in any nation-to-nation conflicts unless there were signs of atrocities or concentration camps established.

Operation Laowai's plan included using one million troops stationed on India's border to mount a massive ground war. The Chinese Army would not send their elite units during the first wave of the attack. They would send "disposable troops" to attack India in order to exhaust India's elite infantry divisions. "Disposable troop" units were formed using a combination of homeless men, jobless, those without families, and ethnic-Chinese populations. They were not accounted for in regular census-taking and their numbers were significant. They would be deployed, as Chinese troops had been during the Korean War, where many were sent into battle without weapons. Those without weapons would pick up the weapons of the dead and wounded and advance forward to attack the enemy.

China's elite divisions would attack after the "Disposables Troops" had been wiped out. Records of the casualties would be adjusted, to provide the appropriate accountability, in reporting losses to the outside world. Mobile crematories were sent to all infantry units to quickly dispose of the thousands of dead bodies. No names were recorded—they just disap-peared.

Losing upwards of a million "Disposables" would help the CCP address the famine. There would be fewer mouths demanding their share of the rice.

Using "Disposable Human Beings" to win wars is not a strategy unique to the CCP.

During the Iraq-Iran War (1980—1988) Iran used children to clear minefields! Reporter for *The New York Times*, Terence Smith, de-scribed the use of child soldiers by Iran to clear minefields.

"Young boys, aged 12-17 years, wore red headbands with the words 'Sar Allah' in Farsi (Warriors of God) and small metal keys that the Ayatollah declared were their tickets to Paradise if they were martyred in their mission. Many were sent into battle against Iraqi tanks without any protection and bound by ropes to prevent desertion.

"They were the first wave, making the way for Iranian tanks by clearing barbed wire and minefields with their bodies."

The exact number of casualties inflicted on Iran and Iraq throughout the war isn't known. It is estimated that between 500,000 to one million were killed and wounded during the eight-year war.

The last time China had gone to war with India was in 1962. The war was started due to India providing asylum to the Dalai Lama and other border issues. Much of the fighting took place in the mountains, and both sides reported casualties in the thousands. These statistics were never verified. Many troops, on both sides, froze to death from the severe cold. The War ended when China declared a ceasefire and withdrew its troops to the China-India border.

The next presenter was Hsu Tzong-Ii, a staff member of Standing Committee member, Wang Huning. Tzong-li had been assigned to provide an update on the progress of Chinese business in Mexico and Brazil.

Tzong-li began, "We have had much success with the governments of Mexico and Brazil. The Presidents of both countries are devoted socialists, and they have welcomed our help in building new infrastructure in their countries. They also have welcomed our agricultural experts to help them increase their crop yields. This will provide greater shipments of food to China."

China's main objective in helping the governments of Mexico and Brazil was to take advantage of each countries' natural resources. China has been in desperate need of these resources.

Mexico's significant resources include iron ore, gold, copper, zinc, silver, and petroleum. Other resources include timber and agricultural products.

Brazil's natural resources include iron ore, manganese, petroleum, timber, steel, fertilizers, plastics, gems, phosphates, and bauxite.

"What about the drug business that was interrupted by the extraterrestrials? Is it a problem for us?" asked Committee Member Xuexiang.

"No. The drug shipments were never profitable for us. They did allow us to control the cartels and government agencies of Mexico. They allowed us to disrupt the United States domestically and cause many social problems for the Americans. The interference of the extraterrestrials came as a benefit to us. We no longer must bear the cost of the logistics of drug manufacturing. We remain even in greater control of the Mexican government leaders," said Tzong-li.

"What about Brazil?" asked Standing Committee Member Qi.

"Brazil welcomes our engineers and agricultural experts. We are sending many of our people to live in Brazil and to eventually become citizens there. Our ten-year plan for Brazil projects us to have full control of the government by year eight. We will then have greater economical and agricultural power in order to support our people," said Tzong-li.

The next presenter, Huang Jong-tsun, was to present an update on European activity.

Chairman Xi interrupted and said, "I don't want to discuss Europe at this time. It is not that important to me. I want to listen to our presentation on the United States."

La Ching-te, a staff member of the Standing Committee Member, Zhao Leji, was tasked with providing an update on the United States.

"2024 is a presidential election year for the United States. They will elect a new president in November. We were successful in helping the Democrats put Biden in power. We were able to affect some of the election results in states that would have gone to Trump.

We thought Biden was a perfect choice for us. We had him and his family under our control. Unfortunately, he was mentally unstable. His son's drug addiction was not helpful to us either, but we were able to accomplish many of our objectives despite their weaknesses.

The field of Democratic candidates is large, but as usual, they are not very capable. The leading candidate, Newsom, is not very intelligent. He has a poor legislative and leadership record in California. The Left-wing of the Democratic Party are very young, lack intelligence, and act immaturely. Old man Sanders looks to be too old for the Democrats to support. They probably will select a homosexual, or a woman, to be their candidate for the national election. We haven't determined which Democrat to support.

"What about Trump?" asked Chairman Xi.

"We believe that Trump will be the Republican candidate for President in 2024," replied La Ching-te.

"If he runs, we must do everything possible to stop him. He must lose. He will be a major problem for us if he becomes President again. We must find another weak person, like Biden, who will not interfere with our global operations," said Xi.

"Yes, Chairman Xi. I will inform the unit that attacked Trump in 2020. I will give them your order to proceed with a plan to stop him."

"Make sure that they are properly funded to accomplish the plan," said Xi.

"Yes Chairman," said La Ching-te.

The only western leader that the Chinese feared was Donald Trump. They feared him, because they knew that he did not fear them. They considered him to be very intelligent, hardworking, and too rich to bribe. Trump had characteristics not typically found in western leaders. He was unpredictable, and he did not have allegiances to any party or group. When he held office, he did not hesitate to make demands of China and its leaders in public, without consulting with them in advance. He did not play the "diplomatic game" and they did not like that—his erratic personality made it impossible for them to control him.

The CCP was delighted when Trump was defeated in the 2020 election, due to the corruption of the voting process in many states. They spent millions supporting left-wing groups and politicians in the United States, in order to rig elections and buy votes. Their efforts allowed them to squeak by with a victory for the Democrats. It was a victory for the CCP as well.

The Chinese have been bribing American politicians since the 1950s. It began with a few, to accomplish small objectives. After President Nixon traveled to China to meet with Chairman Mao in 1972, the Chinese began pursuing American politicians aggressively. By the 1980s, their "elite capture" of American politicians had grown significantly.

The Democratic politicians were the easiest to approach and later coerce. They were always promoting social issues and seeking funds. Chinese operatives were always there to support and provide funds. The Chinese would get in at a modest level and then add greater financial support as they obtained greater control over the politician.

Even though the CCP openly complained and made threats over the loss of their nuclear weapons capability, due to the efforts of Jim and the Source, they were privately pleased. Their calculations determined that a nuclear conflict would not be advantageous for them and could be terminal. Their plan to dominate the world did not include a nuclear war. With the loss of the world's nuclear weapons capability, it was now easier and less costly for them to continue to implement their twenty-year plan.

The CCP has a detailed strategy to overtake the United States as the world's dominant power. Their plan expects to reach that goal by the year 2049—the one-hundred-year anniversary of China's revolution.

Ever since China had been allowed to join the World Trade Organization (WTO) on December 11, 2001, they have been pursuing the domination of the world. They have been acquiring western capital, technology, and natural resources to fuel their own modernization.

The CCP has been secretly purchasing thousands of acres of American farmland. They are using surrogate companies to purchase the land to avoid public outcry. Some of the land is located near United States Military installations, causing a security risk to the Nation.

The United States, and other western countries, have spent billions of dollars developing China and its state-owned businesses. At the same time, China has spent millions of dollars stealing western intelligence property and undermining western countries' elections and peaceful transfers of power.

Today, the CCP has become the major financial source for Hollywood movie producers. Their funding allows them to influence and censor any productions that might reflect negatively on the CCP government.

The National Basketball Association (NBA) has a $5 billion-dollar business in China. A few of the principal team owners have assets close to $10 billion tied up in China. Even though 74% of the NBA players are black, they have turned a "blind eye" and remain silent about the concentration camps and slave operations of two million people of color.

The CCP has targeted American Universities as a prime source for scientific, technical, engineering research, and innovation. They have established campus-based Confucius Institutes of propaganda to attract high-end foreign scientists, engineers, and managers. They have "elite-captured" many American university professors with substantial compensation to promote communism/socialism in order to influence the student population.

Western high-tech companies have given away trade secrets and intellectual property to the CCP in the naïve hope that they would have free access to China's huge domestic market—China will never grant free access to their domestic markets.

"America sleeps" while China marches on towards their goal of world domination.

# CHAPTER TWO

# THE RAPE TREE

One mile southwest of McAllen, Texas, a group of immigrants from Guatemala huddled together for the night. It was early evening, close to 8 o'clock. There was very little visibility—only the moonlight. Four Mexican smuggler-guides sat twenty feet away from the Guatemalans and were in a heated discussion that the group could not hear clearly or understand. The smugglers were arguing over whom to choose and how many. They planned to separate certain women and girls from the group and molest them.

McAllen is the largest city in Hildago County, Texas. It is the twenty-second largest city in Texas. The city is located at the southern tip of the state, in the Rio Grande Valley, on the Mexico-United States border.

The climate of McAllen is sub-tropical. It has very hot, muggy summers and mild winters with short cold spells. From April to October, temperatures may range from the high eighties to over 100 degrees Fahrenheit.

When established in 1904, the area around the city was largely rural and agricultural. With the signing of the North American Free Trade Agreement in 1994, the local economy shifted from agriculture to international trade, retail, and tourism.

The McAllen Foreign-Trade Zone (FTZ) was the first foreign-trade zone established in the United States. Many foreign companies take advantage of the **"Maquiladora"** program.

**A Maquiladora is a company located in a foreign-trade zone that allows factories to be largely duty free and tariff-free. These factories take raw materials and assemble, manufacture, or process them. They export the finished product. These factories capitalize on a cheaper labor force and certain tax advantages under the FTZ Agreement.**

The Guatemalan group consisted of twenty-eight people. The group was comprised of three elderly men and two elderly women, over the age of sixty-five. Four young boys and five young girls, all below the age of twelve. Eight women ranging in age from sixteen to thirty and six men, ages seventeen to twenty-eight.

The Republic of Guatemala is a country in Central America. It is bordered by Mexico to the north and west, Belize to the northeast, Honduras to the east, and El Salvador to the southeast. The center of the Maya civilization was in the territory now known as Guatemala. It has a population of seventeen million and is the most populous country in

Central America. More than two million children in Guatemala do not attend school. Many of the children are indigenous girls living in rural areas. Child labor in Guatemala is higher than anywhere else in Latin America. More than half of the population lives below the poverty line and many children cannot afford to go to school.

Guatemala is considered a developing economy, dependent on agriculture. Their traditional crops are coffee, sugar, and bananas.

The four Mexican smuggler-guides were Luis Perez, Jose Alvados, Manual Lopez, and Jorge Varela. They were members of the Los Zetas Cartel and had been smuggling immigrants from Central America and Mexico into the United States over the last three years. All four were in their early twenties, with many tattoos. Each carried a pistol on his belt. They were from the state of Tamaulipas, one of the thirty-one states along with Mexico City, that comprise the 32 Federal states of Mexico.

Their leader, Luis Perez, had completed the eighth grade in Nuevo Laredo. The others had dropped out of grammar school after a few years. Three had prison records for minor theft and robbery. Perez had served two years in a local prison for robbery and the beating of a nightclub owner. While in prison, Perez, was recruited by inmates, to join the Los Zetas.

**The Los Zetas cartel is regarded as one of the most dangerous and brutal cartels in Mexico. They are known for cruel and violent acts, such as beheadings, torture, and murder. Their headquarters are based in Nuevo Laredo, Tamaulipas, across the border from the city of Laredo, Texas.**

After much arguing and negotiating, the cartel members had chosen their victims and had begun separating the females from the main group of

Guatemalans. They chose three women who were in their twenties and one pretty, twelve-year-old girl.

Luis Perez was the cruelest of the four smugglers. He was 5'6" tall and had a baby face. He had dark, piercing eyes. His companions sometimes referred to him as handsome, "El Guapo," but only when they knew he was in a good mood, and they thought they could ingratiate themselves to him. Most of the time, they were in fear of him.

Perez stayed to guard the Guatemalan group while his fellow smugglers led the four females away. He ordered the smugglers to save the young girl for him. They were not to touch her.

"Keep the young fresh one for me," he demanded. He walked among the Guatemalans while examining his pistol, so that they could all see that he was armed. The six Guatemalan men in the group were completely cowed by the mean-looking and fierce-talking Mexicans. None of them had the courage to interfere on behalf of the women, children, or even each other.

When they were no longer in sight, the three smugglers bound the wrists of the females and put duct tape over their mouths. When they came to a large oak tree, they tied the females' wrists to the branches. The three smugglers went in different directions to scout out a comfortable place for themselves. After ten minutes, each smuggler untied and took a female away from the tree. They left the young girl tied to a branch. Each of the three men raped a woman, and then traded her to one of their partners for a second raping. When Manuel Lopez was finished with his second rape, he left to replace Perez, who was guarding the Guatemalans.

Luis Perez had a history of being sadistic and cruel to women. He enjoyed punishing his victims and seeing the terror in their eyes while he was engaged in assaulting them. He always became sexually aroused when he was brutalizing them, especially when they screamed in pain.

Cristela Ramos was twelve years old and had a very pretty face. She had never attended school because her family was too poor. She had been sent, by her mother, to join the Guatemalan group traveling to the United States. She hoped that her daughter would have a chance for a better life. Her mother was a widow and had five other children. Her father had been a drunk and had died two years before from cirrhosis of the liver, leaving the family to fend for themselves. After his death, they had no income. Cristela was sent to the group along with two of her male cousins, Adelmo and Bastian, who were eight and nine-years old. Their families had no money to pay for the trip, but the cartel members recruiting the children were not concerned. They had many customers in Mexico willing to pay a lot of money for the children, especially if they had attractive faces.

During the long journey, Cristela often hugged and comforted her cousins. At night, when they were afraid and cried out for their mother, she told them that everything would be alright. She would also share some of her food with them, after they had quickly devoured theirs and began begging for more.

Cristela was very afraid and began crying as Perez led her to one of the rest areas a short distance from the tree. She had never been with a man before and didn't understand what was happening. He yelled at her to stop crying and when she didn't; he slapped her face several times and punched her in the stomach.

He ripped off her pants and tore away her panties. He forced himself into her vagina. The pain was so severe that she almost fainted. She screamed and sobbed. Her screams were muffled by the duct tape that was taped tightly over her mouth. When Perez was finished with her, he yelled to Jose Alvalos to bring him one of the older women. When Jose arrived, Perez ordered Jose to take the little one away. He said, "I want a real woman now." He pointed to the woman with Jose and asked, "How was she with you?"

Jose replied, "She's good. She doesn't fight. She likes to be fucked!"

Jose returned Cristela to the Guatemalan group. She was bleeding, bruised, and in shock. The two elderly women in the group hugged her and tried to comfort her. The three elderly men in the group turned their eyes away from the women and said nothing. They were afraid and ashamed.

Before the smugglers returned the three women and young girl to the Guatemalan group, they took articles of clothing from each of them. Luis found the panties that he had ripped off Cristela. They were his trophy, and he tied them to a tree branch. Others took the women's bras or panties. As they were leaving, the smugglers tied the underwear to the branches of the oak tree. The underwear was a trophy and their way of demonstrating their power. They took pictures with their cell phones to show and brag to their friends at home.

Over the last six months, the four Mexican human smugglers had trafficked three hundred and fifty immigrants from Central America into the United States.

Of the three hundred and fifty, they had raped and brutalized sixty-two women and young girls. One of the young girls was nine years old.

The smugglers had been well compensated for their human trafficking. One months' share of the profit for bringing the immigrants into the

United States was more money than they could earn in Mexico, in ten years, while working a regular job.

Unfortunately, the rape of the three women and young girl, by the smugglers of the Los Zetas cartel, was not the end of their misery. After being turned over to a new group of human smugglers in Texas, the three women, along with two others, were raped again in a stash house near Falfurrias, Texas.

Twelve-year-old Cristela Ramos had been spared this time, as she was still bleeding and bruised with a swollen black-eye. Her appearance was not very appealing to the new smugglers. Some of the Guatemalan women in the group had been raped on five different occasions since leaving their homeland to travel through Mexico on the way to their destination in the United States.

*New York Times* reporter Manny Fernandez published an article on March 3, 2019, entitled, **"Braving Heat and Coyotes to be Raped at Border."**

He reported that a 36-year-old mother of three had just completed the journey from her native Guatemala, crossing the Rio Grande on a raft before being led to a house in the Texas border city of McAllen. She said that for weeks she was locked in a room and that the men she had paid to get her safely to the United States had drugged her with pills and cocaine, refusing to let her out of the room even to bathe.

"They raped us so many times they didn't see us as human beings anymore," she said.

Fernandez also reported that, "What was less understood is that the violence that befalls migrant women happens not just during the perilous journey through Mexico. Much of it happens after women reach the supposed safety of the United States."

In 2017, a guide leading a group of migrants through the Tohono O'odham Nation's reservation in Arizona raped a woman from El Salvador twice during a seven-day desert hike. He threatened to leave her stranded if she resisted. The woman told authorities that he said, "I hope I leave you pregnant, so you have one of my kids."

Elizabeth Goldberg, of Fusion Media Group, a division of Univision Communications, reported that the number of Central American women and girls crossing into the United States had been increasing. Her report estimated that eighty percent of women and girls crossing into the United States, by way of Mexico, were raped during their journey.

**"Rape had been perpetrated by guides, fellow migrants, bandits or government officials. Sometimes sex was used as a form of payment, when women and girls did not have money to pay bribes."**

Fusion's reporting on the raping of Central American women and girls was confirmed by David Sivak, Fact Check Editor.

A Pew Research study reported that the number of unaccompanied Central American girls caught at the border had outpaced the number of boys.

# CHAPTER THREE

# THE POISONING OF AMERICA

Jim Vincent, a retired business owner from Silicon Valley and former captain in the Army, had retired to his ranch in Napa, California. He had been visited by an extraterrestrial calling itself The Source. Extraterrestrials had been observing activity on the Earth for decades. They had begun closer observations of the Earth after the detonation of the first nuclear bomb, by Americans, on July 16, 1945. The detonations had sent shock waves into space and had reached other planets. The Extraterrestrials had become concerned about the nuclear technological developments on Earth.

The Extraterrestrials visited the Earth to address the evils of the world.

After their first meeting, Vincent and The Source had agreed to partner in the pursuit of eliminating evil threats to mankind. They first addressed the social media companies that censored users and violated the tenets of the American Constitution. They then chose to eliminate nuclear weapons of mass destruction, from all nations of the world, in order to avoid an event of global annihilation.

Jim and The Source didn't pause very long before choosing their next targets. They chose the global opioid epidemic and the crime wave plaguing the cities of America. To have the most powerful country in the world engulfed in rampant street crime in their largest cities was a dangerous signal to the rest of the world. The United States had been weakened in the eyes of the world due to the uncontrolled crime and failure to secure the southern border against the invasion of illegal immigrants from over one hundred countries. Communities were being destroyed by street gangs, drug addicts, and the deadly drug fentanyl. The inner cities had been turned into "killing fields," as millions of illegal immigrants crossed over the southern border, with impunity, into the United States.

The world had woken up to Jim's outsized influence on how things were done, and he had more enemies than he knew.

He and The Source had orchestrated attacks that had destroyed the cocaine processing plants in Mexico and Central America. They had intercepted, and prevented, the movement of the Mexican Drug Cartel's cash, bound to be laundered, by Hong Kong banks. The laundered money had been deposited in Hong Kong bank accounts for the benefit of the drug cartels.

Carlos Salinas was the most powerful banker in Mexico. He had been providing the cartels with the hidden channel to the Hong Kong banks. He was responsible for laundering their cash and had been taking a substantial cut of the laundered money for himself.

Now, the cartels were alarmed with the loss of their millions in cash and the attacks on their processing plants. They had turned against Salinas and held him responsible for their losses. They threatened his life and gave him very little time to solve the problem. Salinas concluded, due to speculation in the media, that Jim Vincent had organized the attacks on the cartels. He knew he had to act quickly in order to stay alive. He had to come up with a plan to eliminate Jim. Jim had to be killed, if Salinas was to live much longer.

Jim and Source Alpha had agreed to resume their daily routine of meeting at 8 am. They had originally used these meetings to develop information and strategies in pursuing a social media company called Twilight. They had also attacked the nations of the world that had nuclear weapons. They communicated through Jim's computer in his home office.

They agreed to address two global evils at a time, planning and executing the necessary strategies in order to eliminate them. They had agreed to maintain their mutual policy of trying to avoid any deaths in accomplishing their missions.

When they first began collaborating, they addressed the threat of the powerful social media companies that were restricting freedom to users of their technology. They also addressed the potential of global annihilation from nuclear weapons in the control of unstable governments.

They had attacked and destroyed the nuclear weapons capability of many countries that had built and maintained nuclear weapons arsenals. They had attacked and neutralized the ability of the social media company, Twilight. Twilight was not able to resume operation until they agreed, and pledged, to no longer censor their users over First Amendment speech.

The attack, and submission of Twilight, had led to other social media companies changing their policies of censoring users. Larger tech companies adopted Twilight's approach, and they worked diligently to avoid censoring the wrong users. They had also stopped contributing to political parties and political action committees, PACs.

Jim and The Source had long ago decided that it would be fruitless to work with governments and their leaders to eradicate evil. They would operate independently. They believed that most governments were corrupt and incompetent. Their leaders were more concerned about maintaining their power than they were about the welfare of their citizens.

Jim's new presentation to Source Alpha focused on global drug trafficking and the current crime wave plaguing the people of the United States. These were the subjects and targets of their next efforts in confronting evil in the world.

The information for Jim's presentations came from his extensive library of research topics and statistics that he had stored on his computer. Over the last twenty-years, Jim had had a monthly practice of storing information that he had read, researched, or viewed on TV documentaries.

There were many topics, and they were wide-ranging. He had compiled files of data about abortion, climate change, FBI crime statistics, the opioid epidemic, and the covid pandemic. He also compiled files on the histories of socialism, communism, liberalism, conservatism, and racism.

He had extensive data on the Republican and Democratic parties. He had profiled many politicians, past and recent presidents, and their administrations. He noted the policies of the different administrations and the political parties and the effect that they have had on domestic and global events, including war.

Jim opened the morning meeting with Source Alpha by listing the current deadliest drugs in America per the Center for Disease Control (CDC).

1) Fentanyl
2) Heroin
3) Cocaine
4) Methamphetamines
5) Alprazolam (Xanax)
6) Oxycodone
7) Morphine
8) Methadone
9) Hydrocodone
10) Diazepam (Valium)

Over 60% of deaths in the United States, from illegal drugs, involved fentanyl, heroin, and cocaine.

"We are going to target the top three killer drugs—fentanyl, heroin, and cocaine. If we can stop the illegal processing, and transporting, of these three, we will save thousands of lives and reduce crime," said Jim. "We will change the economics of the drug world significantly."

"I will ask Source Bravo to join us in these discussions. Source Bravo will provide the best support to you in pursuing these targets," said Source Alpha.

"That would be great. In order to destroy the illegal drug trafficking, we will use similar tactics and technologies, just as we used against the high-tech company and the nations that possessed nuclear weapons," replied Jim.

Source Bravo joined the meeting the following morning and Jim conducted detailed presentations about each of the three drugs and their origins.

Jim's presentation began with a discussion of the three deadliest illegal drugs:

**Fentanyl** – According to the U.S. – China Economic and Security Review Commission, China is the primary country of origin for illicit fentanyl and fentanyl-related substances trafficked into the United States. Chinese traffickers use various strategies to circumvent regulations, including chemical precursors, and are changing some of their manufacturing schemes to avoid detection. Chinese brokers launder Mexican drug money through China's financial system: Chinese money launderers are using financial technology, mobile apps, and social media to evade authorities.

The manufacturing and export of illicit fentanyl shipments from China were conducted under the purview of the Chinese Communist Party (CCP). Chinese drug brokers operated with the knowledge, support, and approval of the CCP. The CCP participated in the financial transactions with the brokers.

India is emerging as a new source of finished fentanyl powder and fentanyl precursor chemicals. In 2018, Chinese traffickers began shifting some of their fentanyl production to India.

Fentanyl overdoses in the United States have surged to become the leading cause of death for adults between the ages of 18 and 45.

From June 2020 to May 2021, there were more than 100,000 deaths in the United States due to drug overdoses. Fentanyl and synthetic opioids accounted for over two-thirds of the deaths.

Fentanyl is trafficked primarily by land across the United States southern border with Mexico. Some cartels have also increased the use of the United States Postal Service to ship their drugs.

Mexico is now the 'dominant source' of the United States' fentanyl supply, and the synthetic opioids that are rapidly saturating the drug markets.

The CDC reported that most overdoses and deaths associated with fentanyl are related to an illicit version of the drug, which is often a mixture involving heroin or cocaine.

Fentanyl is sometimes laced with heroin and is manufactured into counterfeit tablets, using brand names such as Adderall and Xanax. Many consumers, not looking for fentanyl, are poisoned by the deadly drugs that are mislabeled with popular brand names.

Deaths due to fentanyl overdoses occur due to respiratory depression or cardiac arrest. The drug slows down the heart rate and lowers the blood pressure.

**Heroin** – Foreign sources of opium are responsible for the entire supply of heroin consumed in the United States. Opium is produced in three regions—Southeast Asia, Southwest Asia, and Latin America. It is a worldwide problem.

In 2020, nearly 14,000 people in the United States died from a drug overdose involving heroin. That is a rate of four deaths for every 100,000 Americans.

A primary cause of death among people who overdose on heroin is hypoxia. This occurs when not enough oxygen is getting to the brain, due to slowed or stopped breathing. Hypoxia can have long-term consequences, including brain damage, coma, and death.

**Cocaine** – Countries in the cocaine trade include those where coca plants are grown and processed. They are Colombia, Bolivia, and Peru. Countries that transport cocaine across national boundaries are Mexico, Haiti, the Bahamas, and the Dominican Republic.

The drug is often transported from Colombia to Mexico or Central America by sea, and then into the United States across land borders. It is estimated that 90% of cocaine transported into the United States comes through the United States and Mexico border. Cocaine comes mostly through the state of Texas. Smaller quantities come across California and Arizona borders.

Cocaine is often cut with adulterants to reduce its purity and create greater profits. Common among cutting agents include amphetamines, baking sugars, caffeine, acetaminophen (Tylenol), cornstarch, flour, talcum powder, and anesthetics, including procaine.

Once the cocaine has arrived in the United States, distributors sell it to wholesale dealers. These dealers sell it to mid-level drug dealers, who, in turn, sell it to low-level street dealers.

Most consumers buy their cocaine from street dealers. Street dealers often employ individuals for roles as transporters (mules), delivery, counters of money, back-up people to watch for law enforcement, and collectors of debt.

Deaths from cocaine overdoses are caused by heart attack, stroke, or seizures. While cocaine increases dopamine and norepinephrine in the brain to create euphoric effects, boosting confidence and focus, it also stimulates the cardiovascular system. These cardiovascular effects are by far the most dangerous and are often what lead to cocaine-induced death.

Jim continued with, "China has become a virtual **'Prison Nation.'**"

In his October 21, 2020, article entitled "China is Killing Americans with Fentanyl—Deliberately," Gordon Chang reported that "The Chinese Communist Party (CCP), through its' cells, controls every business of any consequence."

Chang's article went on to explain that **"The Chinese central government operates what is undoubtedly the world's most sophisticated set of social controls. Using bid data and artificial intelligence, tens of thousands of government watchers surveil 1.4 billion people with approximately 626 million surveillance cameras and tens of millions of neighborhood monitors and Communist Party cadres. Beijing tightly controls the banking system and knows of money transfers instantaneously."**

"So, when a Chinese National gifted Hunter Biden with a 3.16-carat diamond estimated to be worth $80,000, or contracted with him for 'introductions alone,' for $10 million a year, for a minimum of three years, the CCP were informed immediately," said Jim.
- Source *New York Post*, Miranda Devine.

"When Hunter Biden joined a Chinese investment firm called Bohai Harvest RST (Shanghai) Equity Investment Fund Management Company to hold a 10% stake, the transaction was approved by the CCP," said Jim.
- Source *Washington Examiner*, Jerry Dunleavy.

Bohai Harvest RST has invested in Chinese Communist Party-linked firms that the United States has sanctioned. The sanctions included a technology company accused of assisting in human rights abuses against the Uyghurs and a nuclear company that allegedly conspired to acquire U.S. nuclear technology in order to benefit China's military.
- Source *Washington Examiner*.

"What are the first steps to take in addressing the deadly Mexican Cartels and the Chinese drug supply? Where do you want to start?" asked Source Bravo.

"I'll detail everything in the next presentation," replied Jim.

# CHAPTER FOUR

# THE ATTACK PLAN

Jim began the afternoon presentation by explaining the reasoning behind their strategy for attacking the cartels and the fentanyl supply from China.

"China has been planning for decades to take the United States down in any way they can. They have concluded that they don't have to go to war with the United States when there are so many other peaceful ways to defeat us. They want to destroy us from within. Corrupting our government officials and providing huge quantities of illegal drugs to destroy the fabric of American society are key elements of their strategy," he said

## THE JOE BIDEN SCANDAL

Communist spies operating, at the highest levels, in the United States government are not new. During the presidential administration of

Franklin Delano Roosevelt (FDR), his closest aid Harry Hopkins was considered a pro-Soviet agent of influence.

According to testimony by Whittaker Chambers, who was a courier for a Soviet spy ring in Washington, Harry Dexter White, a key advisor to Treasury Secretary Henry Morgenthau, passed classified information to him.

Most advanced nations spy on each other for various reasons—even friendly nations spy on friendly nations.

The uncovering of the Joe Biden corruption scandal was important, different, and more significant than other scandals because the Chinese Communist Party (CCP) was able to penetrate the inner offices of the Obama White House by bribing, and coercing, greedy Americans.

Once the Chinese had coerced the vice president and his relatives, it cannot be realistically expected that the coercion stopped with them.

There has been no further official accounting of the number of White House personnel, or employees of other Federal Agencies, that might have been coerced as well, due to the corrupt activities of the vice president.

It was extraordinary for a sitting vice president, his brother, and his drug addicted son to contract with Chinese operatives, Ukrainians, and citizens of other nations for millions of dollars.

When the son traveled to China on Air Force 2 with his father, it gave the signal to the CCP that they were not only open to, but were looking for personal business opportunities.

When the CCP paid money to the son, they knew the funds were also going to his father.

When the vice president, in an open press conference, arrogantly withheld $1 billion in aid to the Ukraine government in order to force the firing of a Ukrainian prosecutor who was investigating his son's partners— it sent a giant signal as well.

The vice president and his associates were selling access to the White

House and foreign operatives were more than willing to purchase the access with large sums of cash, loans, and huge lucrative contracts.

In the example of the CCP—their operatives met and contracted with the vice president, his family, and associates, for the purpose of purchasing access to the highest levels of the government at the expense of the American people.

All Chinese operatives report directly to the Chinese Communist Party (CCP). No deals of any kind are consummated without the approval of the CCP. The successful Chinese operatives celebrated like it was the Chinese New Year and they had been promoted due to their accomplishing the CCP's objectives of spying on high levels of the United States government. They had never accomplished an "Elite Capture" of an enemy at such a high level before.

A Federal Investigation is still ongoing into the activities of Joe Biden, his family, and associates.

Two fundamental questions need to be answered. Did Biden and his associates provide aid and comfort to America's enemies in selling access to our government's activities? Did Biden betray the trust of the American people in using his elected office to obtain illicit wealth?

## MORE SPIES

In 2018, the FBI notified Senator Dianne Feinstein, a Democrat from California, now 89-years-old and the oldest sitting United States Senator, that a member of her staff was a Chinese spy. The spy had been employed by her for over twenty-years. He was listed as an "office director" on payroll records and served as her driver when she was in San Francisco. He was also reporting to China's Ministry of State Security through China's San Francisco Consulate.

"Feinstein, allegedly, forced him to retire, after twenty-years!" said Jim.

Jeff Harp, former FBI agent and KPIX security analyst, reported that, "The Chinese spies are often focused on things like R&D, technology, and trade secrets. They also have an interest in the economy here. How to get political influence here. What's being developed in Silicon Valley that has dual-use technology? When it comes to counterintelligence and espionage, the Bay Area is the trendsetter. All of this is tied to the Bay Area in California. As the Bay Area goes, so does the nation when it comes to technology. So why not when it comes to spying?"

Feinstein's husband, Richard Blum, died on February 27, 2022. Blum was her third husband, and they had been married for forty-two years. Public records show a venture capital firm, backed by Blum's investment bank, owned millions in stock in corporations doing business with China.

Blum's firm was Newbridge Capital, a joint venture between Richard C. Blum & Associates and another firm called Texas Pacific Group. It maintained an office in Shanghai for an affiliate called Newbridge Asia.

Blum and Feinstein had been criticized for making millions of dollars from votes and decisions that she made in the Senate. Feinstein's votes for military contracts during the Iraq and Afghanistan wars directly benefited Blum's investments.

Fang Fang, also known as Christine Fang, was a Chinese National operating as a spy in the United States for the Chinese Communist Party (CCP). She posed as a student between the years 2011 and 2015. She targeted rising Democratic political stars who seemed to be destined for national political roles.

She was guided in her activities by a Chinese National, under diplomatic cover, in the San Francisco consulate. According to sources of Axios, she also received instructions directly from Beijing.

The New York Post reported in 2020 that, "Fang was a Chinese Mata Hari—who allegedly slept with at least two Midwestern mayors while cozying up to a slew of pols across the country in a bid to infiltrate the U.S. political system."

"She was on a mission," a U.S. counter-intelligence official said of Fang—and it included plenty of seduction before the feds got wind of her antics and she vanished in 2015.

The idea was for Fang to maneuver herself into key government circles—and sometimes politicians' beds—to gain personal information about them while ingratiating herself with unwitting potential up-and-coming heavy-hitters, intelligence sources told *Axios*.

The *New York Post* reported that United States officials know of at least two mayors who had romantic relationships with Fang, lasting about three years.

The accused spy had sex with an Ohio mayor in a car. "The incident was caught on FBI electronic surveillance," an intelligence official said. The mayor had asked Fang, at one point, why she was into him. She allegedly replied that she needed to improve her English.

She became the head of a Chinese student association in the Bay Area of California and used fundraiser events and rallies to get close to political candidates.

Fang is said to have first met Democratic Congressman Eric Swalwell when he was a council member in Dublin City, California.

*Fox News* anchor Tucker Carlson claimed that U.S. Intelligent agencies believed that Swalwell had been in a sexual relationship with Fang Fang.

According to a report by *Axios*, Swalwell cut off his contact with Fang after he received a "defensive briefing" from FBI agents who were investigating her.

She was also reputed to have raised cash in 2013 for Democrat, Tulsi Gabbard, of Hawaii.

Fang had volunteered to campaign for Democratic Representative Ro Khannah's 2014 run for Congress. He was elected two years later.

Peter Schweizer, President of Government Accountability Institute (GAI) and a Breitbart News senior contributor recently published, *Red-Handed: How American Elites Get Rich Helping China Win.*

His book revealed how twenty-three United States senators and congressman have lobbied for Chinese military or intelligence-linked companies after leaving office.

He reported that, "Many law makers cash in after leaving office by becoming lobbyists for corporations and other special interests." Schweizer's book revealed that many former congressional leaders, committee chairman, and rank-and-file members are lobbying for Chinese intelligence and military-linked companies.

## ELITE CAPTURE

"Elite capture is a form of corruption whereby public resources are biased for the benefit of a few individuals of superior social status in detriment to the welfare of the larger population. This specific form of corruption occurs when elites use public funds, originally intended to be invested in services that benefit the larger population, to fund projects that would only benefit them."

The Chinese Communist Party (CCP) has its own "Long Game" strategy to replace America's dominance.

Michael Pillsbury's, *The Hundred-Year Marathon*, suggests that there is much evidence showing the Chinese government has a detailed strategy to overtake the United States as the world's dominant power.

A subset strategy of the CCP's long-term strategy to dominate the world is "Elite Capture."

Peter Schweizer explained that, "China views itself as in a competition with the United States. President Xi, of China, had been talking about that since 2012, and they have decided that the way they can win is not going toe to toe with this dynamic economy and culture. China believes it can win by buying off the elites. They call it elite capture."

The most prominent example of "elite capture" by the CCP, has been the Joe Biden family. Just prior to the general election in 2020, new revelations had come to light for the American people that the Biden family had been receiving extraordinary sums from CCP operatives. Evidence continued to come forth that the Biden family, specifically Joe Biden, his brother Jim, and his son Hunter, had been directly involved with the Chinese. They had been "elite captured" by the CCP.

Tony Bobulinski, a former business partner of Joe, Jim, and Hunter Biden, informed the FBI in 2020 that Joe Biden was the "Chairman" and a "figurehead" of the Bidens' overseas business dealings.

In an interview with Tucker Carlson, on "Tucker Carlson Tonight," televised on October 3, 2022, Bobulinski stated that there were hundreds of data points that Joe Biden was acting in—in a capitalistic term, the chairman of the Biden family businesses while vice president of the United States.

The Biden family had been involved in business transactions amounting to hundreds of millions of dollars, with individuals who had direct ties to Chinese intelligence, while Joe Biden was vice president of the United States, and since then.

## THE CHINESE COMMUNIST PARTY (CCP) RECRUITMENT PROGRAM TO "CAPTURE AMERICAN ELITES"

Peter Schweizer's recent book listed the following twenty-three former members of Congress who have lobbied for Chinese military or intelligence-linked companies.

**Former Speaker of the House John Boehner (R-OH)** - Boehner joined the law firm, Squire Patton Boggs (SPB), as a "strategic advisor." SPB registered as a foreign agent of the Chinese embassy in Washington, D.C., after decades of close ties to the Chinese government. SPB advised and helped Beijing navigate "issues that will threaten their interests."

**Senator Tim Hutchinson (R-AR)** - a former member of the Senate Armed Services Committee, lobbied for Alibaba, the Chinese technology giant. Alibaba paid his firm, Greenberg Traurig $200,000 in 2020.

**Representative Rodney Frelinghuysen (R-NJ)** - Greenberg Traurig hired Frelinghuysen to lobby on behalf of Chinese companies.

**Representative Albert Wynn (D-MD)** - Greenberg Traurig hired Wynn to lobby on behalf of Chinese companies.

**Representative Ed Royce (R-CA)** - Tencent is a massive Chinese technology company and the creator of WeChat, a popular Chinese messaging app with over 1.2 billion active monthly users. Tencent also develops technologies with military applications and is closely "fused" with China's Ministry of Public Security and the People's Liberation Army. Tencent hired former House Foreign Affairs Committee Chairman Ed Royce to lobby the federal government. Tencent paid his firm $330,000 in 2020.

**Former Senate Majority Leader Trent Lott (R-MS)** – ByteDance is a large Chinese company that operates TikTok, the social media supersuccess that has been widely criticized for its privacy, censorship practices, as well as its close ties to the Chinese government. ByteDance hired Lott to lobby on their behalf. The American think tank, Peterson Institute for International Economics, described TikTok as a "Huawei-sized problem" that posed a national security threat to the United States.

**Senator John Breaux (D-L.A.)** – Senator Breaux was hired by ByteDance to lobby on their behalf. Breaux once remarked that his vote in the Senate was not for sale, but it is "available for rent."

**Representative Jeff Denham (R-CA)** – ByteDance hired Denham to lobby the federal government on their behalf.

**Representative Bart Gordon (D-TN)** – ByteDance hired Gordon to lobby the federal government on their behalf.

**Senator Norman Coleman (R-MN)** – ZTE Corporation, a military-linked Chinese telecommunications firm, hired Coleman to lobby the federal government on their behalf. ZTE paid Coleman's firm $2.94 million in 2019. The FCC has declared ZTE telecom hardware a "national security" threat.

**Senator Joe Lieberman (D-CT)** – ZTE hired Lieberman, the former vice-presidential candidate in 2000, to lobby the federal government on their behalf.

**Representative Jon Christensen (R-NE)** – ZTE hired Christensen to lobby the federal government on their behalf.

**Representative Connie Mack (R-FL)** – ZTE hired Mack to lobby the federal government on their behalf.

**Representative Don Bonker (D-WA)** – Huawei, is a Chinese multinational technology corporation. It designs, develops, produces, and sells telecommunications equipment, consumer electronics, and smart devices. Huawei hired Bonker to lobby the federal government on their behalf. Bonker has been employed by the lobbying firm APCO Worldwide.

**Representative Cliff Stearns (R-FL)** – Huawei hired Stearns to lobby the federal government on their behalf. Stearns has been employed by the lobbying firm APCO Worldwide.

**Representative Lee Terry (R-NE)** – Huawei hired Terry in 2021 to lobby the federal government on their behalf. The FCC has declared Huawei telecom hardware a "national security" threat.

**Representative Jack Kingston (R-GA)** – ChemChina, the Chinese state-owned chemical company, hired Kingston to lobby the federal government on their behalf. Kingston had been a long-time member of the Defense Appropriations Subcommittee.

**Senator David Vitter (R-L.A.)** – Hikvision, a Chinese surveillance company, is owned by the government-controlled conglomerate known as the Chinese Electronics Group. Hikvision hired Vitter to lobby the federal government. He received a payment of $70,000 per month for his lobbying efforts.

**Representative Toby Moffett (D-CT)** – Hikvision also paid Moffett $70,000 per month to lobby the federal government on their behalf.

**Representative Rick Boucher (D-VA)** – Hikvision hired Boucher's firm and paid them $1.75 million in 2019, for lobbying on behalf of Hikvision.

**Senator Barbara Boxer (D-CA), former vice chair of the Select Committee on Ethics** – Hikvision hired Boxer as an adviser. She registered as a foreign agent with the Department of Justice. Later, after much public outcry, Boxer stopped lobbying for Hikvision.

**Representative Charles Boustany (R-L.A.)** – After 12 years in Congress, Boustany joined Capitol Counsel, a Washington D.C. lobbying firm. Capitol Counsel registered with the Department of Justice as a foreign agent to represent the China-United States Exchange Foundation (CUSEF). As part of this contract with CUSEF, Capitol Counsel provided "political intelligence gathering" and "substantive advice on China-related legislation," including arranging meetings on Capitol Hill. Boustany also became a spokesperson for an organization called Tariffs Hurt the Heartland, which argued that the Trump administration's proposed tariffs on China's abusive trade practices would hurt working-class Americans.

**Senator William Cohen (R-ME)** – Former Senator and Defense Secretary in the Clinton administration, Cohen, was hired by Huawei. The federal government deemed Huawei a security threat, because of its close ties to the Chinese intelligence apparatus. Huawei hired Cohen to negotiate with the United States director of national intelligence to find a way to sell its hardware in the United States. Cohen also provided consulting services for Chinese state-owned enterprises, "often used as tools of the Chinese state."

**Peter Schweizer has called for a ban on lobbying on behalf of Chinese military and intelligence-linked companies.**

Mary Dowling, of *The Independent Sentinel*, reported in 2019 that the Trump Administration added Chinese-owned Huawei Technologies to a trade blacklist.

**"The CCP placed Huawei equipment atop cell towers on purchased farmland near U.S. military bases in the Midwest. The FBI said the equipment can capture and disrupt communications, that is, by U.S. Strategic Command which oversees the country's nuclear weapons."**

"This gets into some of the most sensitive things we do," said one former FBI official with knowledge of the investigation. "It would impact our ability for essentially command and control with the nuclear triad."

The Trump Administration warned about the danger of potential Chinese spies buying land near U.S. Army bases.

"CNBC reported that the CCP bought a farm in North Dakota near a U.S. Air Force Drone base. The CCP must think us to be incredibly stupid."

A Chinese Communist firm also bought 130,000 acres in Texas near military bases.

The Center for Disease Control (CDC) announced on November 17, 2021, that, **"Drug Overdose Deaths in the U.S. Top 100,000 Annually."**

Provisional data from CDC's National Center for Health Statistics indicate that there were an estimated 100,306 overdose deaths in the United States during the twelve-month period ending in April 2021, an increase of 28.5% from 78,056 deaths during the same period the year before.

The CDC press release also included, **"Overdose deaths from synthetic opioids (primarily fentanyl) and psychostimulants such as methamphetamine also increased in the 12-month period ending April 2021."**

Jim went to the whiteboard on the wall in his office, where he had taped a map of Mexico and Central America. He pointed to the map as he responded to Source Bravo's questions.

"I suggest that we begin a three-pronged attack on drug trafficking and illegal immigration that the cartels have been taking advantage of in order to carry and divert the flow of their drug shipments. We must put a halt to the stream of thousands of immigrants coming through the southern border of the United States. First, we'll focus on Mexico and the three countries that make up what is referred to as 'The Northern Triangle.'

"The triangle is made up of Guatemala, Honduras, and El Salvador. They have become destabilized and have been transformed into havens for illegal drug trade for the Mexican cartels.

"Guatemala has an ungoverned border with Mexico that makes it a prime location for the thriving drug trade. The lack of law enforcement on the border allows the Mexican cartels, specifically Los Zetas and Sinaloa cartels, to operate with impunity.

"Guatemala had transported over 60% of drugs, in transit, from South American drug producing countries, to the United States.

"The Mexican Sinaloa Cartel has set up a cocaine processing lab on a coffee farm in Honduras. It can produce one ton of cocaine per month.

"We must begin attacking the drug processing plants and, at the same time, stop the illegal cash flow from Mexico to China.

"The drugs are packaged at the processing plants, and that's where we must destroy them. Once the packaged drugs leave the processing plants, they are harder to track down. That's why we must destroy them at the plant locations.

"Cartel cash from drug sales is warehoused on pallets at the airport before being loaded onto international flights bound for China. We must destroy the cash while it is in the warehouses.

"Once we have neutralized the countries of the northern triangle, by destroying their drug processing plants, we will focus on other countries in the region that are also sources for illegal drugs," said Jim.

"Won't there be a strong retaliation when you begin shutting down countries and destroying the cartels cash?" asked Source Bravo.

"Yes. You can count on it. They will try to harm me, my family, and my friends if they are given the opportunity. We must be prepared to respond to their attacks and neutralize their efforts," said Jim.

# CHAPTER FIVE

# BANKER TO THE CARTELS

Carlos Salinas was very intelligent and sophisticated. He was also filled with hate. After graduating from the Universidad Nacional de Mexico in Mexico City, his wealthy Uncle Juan encouraged him to get his master's degree in the United States. Carlos chose to attend the Wharton School of Business at the University of Pennsylvania. Uncle Juan paid for all his expenses.

Carlos was stocky, 5'4" tall and very dark-skinned. He was born in Vera Cruz. Many members of his family were also dark-skinned. He was an excellent soccer player growing up in Mexico, and very popular with the local girls. When he played soccer during the summer months, his skin became even darker, and it sometimes appeared black.

When he played intramural soccer in college, in Pennsylvania, some of his white teammates nicknamed him "beaner" or "shadow." He laughed at their name-calling, but deep-down their comments hurt his feelings. He couldn't stand to be ridiculed. He kept his feelings to himself, but he vowed that he would get back at them someday.

He attempted to date two beautiful, blonde, white girls at the University, but was rejected by both. One of the girls told him, in a joking and cruel manner, that she thought he was a nice guy, but her father would kill her if he found out that she had dated an illegal. The other white girl was polite to him, but always refused his requests for a date.

Later, when he had become a powerful banker for the cartels, he felt no guilt at being involved with the illegal drug trade or with his involvement with the drugs being shipped into the United States.

He didn't care about the human cost of drug abuse. He secretly enjoyed the idea of getting-back at white people, especially the wealthy college students who were consuming large quantities of the drugs. As far as he was concerned, the more American college kids who were dying from overdosing on drugs, the better. Especially if they were white and had died from drugs supplied through his drug operations.

Now, the drug cartel leaders were pressuring him to come up with a solution to stop the attacks on their cocaine processing plants and the destruction of their warehouses, full of cash, bound for Hong Kong.

The media was full of stories about an elderly man who claimed to have a partnership with extraterrestrials. Somehow, they had destroyed the ability of nations to have nuclear weapons. There was also a story about the social networking company that had been shut down. The company was Twilight. Allegedly, it had been forced by this old man to declare that they would not censor their users.

Salinas used his extensive network of law firms and informants in the United States and Mexico to learn more about this old-man, Jim Vincent. He learned that Vincent owned a ranch and vineyards in Napa, California. He was informed by his Mexican American law firm in Los Angeles that, like most vineyard owners, Vincent hired independent contractors to harvest his grapes. The contractors typically hired Mexican Nationals to perform the labor.

The real profit in the wine-making industry was not realized in the making of wine or through the distribution of sales. The greatest profits were generated by owning the vineyards and selling the grapes. Some of the vineyard-owners in the Napa Valley had acres of grape vines valued at $1 million, or more, an acre.

Salinas' law firm in Los Angeles was able to locate the owner of the grape harvesting company that contracted with Jim Vincent. The company, Northern Cal Vineyard Management, was owned by a Mexican-American named Arturo Hernandez. Hernandez lived with his family in Napa and his office was in Vallejo, 14 miles south of Napa.

Salinas called the manager of his L.A. law firm, Jaime Fernandez, and ordered him to investigate Arturo Hernandez. He wanted the investigation to be confidential, and he wanted the report back to him immediately.

"Find out where his relatives are living in Mexico and how often he visits them? Does he have relatives living in the United States? I want to know if he is married and if he has any children. I want to know if he has a mistress. I want to know everything about Hernandez," Salinas instructed.

Fernandez had met Salinas when they both attended the Universidad Nacional de Mexico in Mexico City. Later, when he graduated from law school, he contacted Salinas, and Salinas promptly hired him. Since Fernandez spoke English fluently, Salinas set him up with an office and staff in Los Angeles and funded his law practice. Fernandez hired two young Mexican American attorneys and three bilingual speaking Mexican American women as office help. Salinas was Fernandez's only client.

Within two weeks, Fernandez sent one of his young attorneys to Salinas' office in Mexico City. The attorney delivered a sealed, detailed report on Arturo Hernandez, his family, and his activities.

The report from the attorney in L.A. was very comprehensive. The following detailed Hernandez's history:

Arturo Hernandez was born in Morelia, Mexico on January 10, 1979. He was the oldest of four sons and three daughters, born to Arturo and Teresa Fernandez.

Morelia is a city in the north-central part of the state of Michoacan, in central Mexico. Michoacan is one of the 32 Federal States in Mexico. In 1828, a newly created state of Michoacan changed the name of the city from Valladolid to Morelia, in honor of Jose Maria Morelos y Pavon.

Jose Maria Morelos (1765—1815) was a Mexican Catholic priest, statesman and military leader who led the Mexican War of Independence movement. He led military campaigns against Spanish rule and was viewed by the royal army as its main rival. Under his leadership, the

Congress of Anahuac was installed in Chilpancingo and declared on November 6, 1813, the independence of Mexico. After several military defeats, Morelos was captured by the royalist army. He was tried by Inquisition, defrocked as a priest, and executed by civil authorities on December 22, 1815.

Built in the sixteenth century, Morelia is an example of the Spanish Renaissance. More than two hundred historical buildings promote the architectural history of the city. Many of these buildings had been built using the region's characteristic pink stone. The city's population is approximately 750,000.

When he was five-years old, Hernandez's parents immigrated to the United States with their seven children. They settled with relatives in Redwood City, California. After going through the process of obtaining citizenship in 1989, his parents and their children became U.S. citizens.

Arturo married Marta Burges on February 10, 2001. They were both twenty-two years old. Marta's family was originally from Jalisco, Mexico. Marta was born in San Jose, California.

Arturo and Marta had three children, all girls. Teresa seventeen-, Belin fourteen- and Marta nine-years-old. They lived in a modest home in Vallejo, California.

Arturo's parents lived in Redwood City. He and Marta both had grandparents, uncles, aunts, and cousins living in the Mexican states of Michoacan and Jalisco.

The report listed the relatives' names and addresses in Mexico.

Arturo was able to start his grape harvesting business in 2010 with loans from his parents. He had been operating his business with six permanent employees and three trucks. He had hired grape harvesters on a seasonable basis. Over the years, with few exceptions, his field workers were Mexican Nationals.

After reading through the report, Salinas called his lawyer, Jaime Fernandez, and asked him to come to his office in Mexico City. "We can have some celebrations and then discuss what to do with your report," said Salinas.

When Fernandez met with Salinas in his office in Mexico City, Salinas quickly got to the point.

"We've got to persuade Hernandez to hire two of our people when he begins work on this guy Vincent's ranch. If we can slip two of our men onto the ranch, as workers, we'll be able to eliminate the problem we have with the destruction of our product in Mexico and Central America. It will also stop the attacks on our cash holdings," said Salinas.

"How are we going to convince Hernandez to hire our men?" asked Fernandez.

"Easy. We'll show him how much we know about his family in the United States and in Mexico. If he wants to keep them safe and alive, he will co-operate," said Salinas.

# CHAPTER SIX

# A NEW MISSION

Returning from a brief vacation to Pebble Beach and Carmel, California, with his life partner, Judith Vennell, Jim called his three childhood friends. They had previously worked with him to inform former President Trump about the activities of Jim, The Source, and government agencies. He invited them to come to the ranch for a barbecue and a meeting to discuss a new mission.

Jim had nicknamed Judith "Peaches," and the nickname "stuck!" Even their children, close friends, and acquaintances referred to her by the nickname.

Bob Dixon, Bill Andrew, and Don Ferenz visited with Jim at the ranch and stayed overnight in the guest cottages.

Jim and the three men had been close friends since the eighth grade. Now in their seventies, they looked forward to the next mission that Jim had planned for them.

They had successfully traveled to Florida to deliver information and videos to former President Trump. They didn't meet with Trump, but Trump's organization treated them very well. They played an awkward round of golf on a Trump Championship golf course—quitting after nine holes. Their visit had also included a tour, conducted by a Trump assistant of the Mar-a-Lago resort.

As they sat around the barbecue and drank their third round of cocktails, Jim announced that he had invited them to the ranch to discuss a new mission. Of course, it was always up to them, whether or not they wanted to participate.

Jim explained. "The Source and I have turned our attention to three new objectives. They are the global drug epidemic, the out-of- control crime wave plaguing the American people, and the invasion of illegal immigrants crossing the southern border.

"Tomorrow morning, we'll meet at the basketball court that I am now using as a conference room. At that time, I'll go through the presentation that The Source and I have created. I'd like each of you to present a portion of the presentation when you travel to Texas to meet with a couple of government groups and powerful ranchers."

"What groups are you talking about?" asked Bob.

"Members of the Governor's office, the top officers of the Texas Rangers, and a few of the largest and most powerful ranch owners. It turns out that a few of the ranchers control a lot of the decision-making in Texas," replied Jim.

"Now you're really looking for action," said Bill. "If you're planning to mess with the drug cartels, you'll be dealing with some very tough characters. Life is meaningless to them. They're much tougher than politicians and government employees. There won't be anything they won't do to try to kill you. You're taking everything to a higher level, Jim. Are you ready for that?"

"We've got that covered, Bill. The Source and I will get to them before they are able to mount a significant response. We want to draw them out and have them pursue us. We'll intercept and destroy them. On the other hand, I'll understand if any of you decide not to be a part of this," replied Jim.

"How do you perceive us being involved in these next escapades?" asked Don. "It's not that I have a busy schedule, but with this new endeavor, I might want to purchase more life insurance."

"Primarily, your mission will be to deliver information from The Source and me. You will also be knowledgeable enough to answer their questions. The Source and I will be monitoring your conversations while you are in Texas. We will be immediately available if you need to contact us," said Jim.

"What are we supposed to do with these people?" asked Bob.

"Tomorrow, I'll be going through the entire presentation. You'll understand, much better, after I've had a chance to explain everything. I'll be providing you with information regarding what we are doing to destroy the cocaine processing plants. Also, information about our intercepting huge pallets of cash in warehouses bound for Hong Kong Banks to be laundered. I'll provide you with our plan to co-ordinate with Texas law enforcement and our targeting of the 'Coyotes' who are guiding illegal immigrants to the southern border," said Jim.

"We're not going to have to play golf, are we?" asked Bill. "My days of going out in public and making a fool of myself are over. I might just as well stay home and listen to Thelma tell me what an idiot I am. At least at home I can sit in front of the TV and pretend that I'm listening to her."

"Texans are famous for their hospitality. There might be some activities that they will invite you to participate in, but no, it won't be golf,"

responded Jim.

"How have you explained our role to them?" asked Bob.

"You are personal messengers from The Source and me. I've been forthcoming with them and have explained that you're my close friends. I've made it clear to them that I only trust the three of you. You see, I want to avoid any publicity from my personally visiting government or state and federal agencies. Unless I've been subpoenaed or officially required to meet with them, I want to avoid all contact. I don't want the press attempting to link our activities with anything political or with any specific politicians," said Jim.

"You can't control them, Jim. The press doesn't have a conscious or a sense of morality. They'd sell their grandmother down the river if it would get them a quick headline," said Bob.

# CHAPTER SEVEN

# THE PRESENTATION

The four friends met in Jim's conference room shortly after breakfast.

"Do any of you need anything before we get started? We'll have coffee, soft drinks, and snacks brought in. We're going to have a lengthy presentation. It will last for three or four hours," said Jim.

Everyone was fine and ready to go, so Jim proceeded to begin the presentation.

He went to the whiteboard that was set up at the end of the conference table. He used his computer to project the presentation onto the board.

"Bob, your description of the press yesterday and their lack of morality was spot on, but let me explain about some 'shit' that the Source and I have uncovered. It will motivate you to meet with the Texans. Have you guys ever heard the term 'Rape Trees?'" asked Jim.

They shook their heads, no.

"Neither had I until I read a few articles on the subject. The Rape Trees have been in existence for more than twenty years. They are primarily in Northern Mexico and in the southern regions of Texas and Arizona. Let me read from one of the reports that we found in our search," said Jim.

Jim read the following from an article by journalists Brandon Darby and Bob Price, entitled "Rape Trees, Dead Migrants and the Consequences of an Unsecured Border."

**"Women and girls from Central America are routinely given birth control or morning-after-pills by their mothers in anticipation of the likely sexual assaults that will occur on their journey to the United States."**

The journalists further explained that females are often raped immediately upon making it to their first stop once they arrive in a Mexican stash house from Guatemala. Then they are shipped to the United States–Mexico border, usually to Reynosa, Mexico, immediately south of McAllen, Texas. In the process of traveling from the first stash house to the second, the women and young girls are often sexually assaulted or raped again by the smuggler or group of smugglers taking them between the two locations. The sexual assaults and rapes often happen again in the second Mexican stash house of their journey.

The females are then trickled into the U.S. across the border and brought to a third stash house in a U.S. border town, usually in or near McAllen, Texas. They are often sexually assaulted or raped again by the operator of the stash house if they are deemed attractive by the criminals operating the facility. They are stockpiled until the cartel wants to send a large load of narcotics across the Rio Grande. The Cartel then sends a large group of humans across in one area and then a large drug load across in another area.

Once the human beings are in Texas, another smuggler then picks up the women and young girls and drives them, with a coyote, to a point along Highway 281. This is just before the Border Patrol checkpoint immediately south of Falfurrias, Texas. The checkpoint is approximately eighty-five miles north of the United States–Mexico border.

The women and young girls exit the vehicle with their coyote and attempt to make their way around the checkpoint. Most of the apprehended illegal migrants say that they were told it would be a thirty-minute hike, and they were given a gallon of water for their trip. The reality is that the hike usually takes three to four days. It is common for the coyote to sexually assault or rape the females on this stretch of the journey as well. These coyotes usually remove an article of clothing from the female they rape, and they tie it tightly to a tree—a rape tree.

Rape trees are common in Brooks County, Texas. Benny Martinez, the Chief Deputy at the Brooks Country Sheriff's Department, was quoted as saying, "These guys are animals. There is an intimidation factor there. If they don't give into the brush guide, the women get beat up."

Rape Trees are also common on the southern border of Arizona.

These "rape trees" are places where cartel members and coyotes rape female border crossers and hang their clothes, specifically undergarments, to mark their conquest.

"You know, when we refer to many of these victims as young girls, we are really talking about children. These women and children have been raped on many occasions during their journey towards the U.S. border. Some attractive females were raped more than five times. We must stop these animals. The Left in America don't care about these human beings. If they did, they would make the effort to understand what is really going on at our southern border and do something about it. But again, they just don't care," said Jim.

"Wow, why doesn't the Mexican government do something about what's going on? It's happening in their country," said Bill.

"Are you kidding? Human life doesn't have much value in Mexico. When we're talking about migrants from Central American countries, the Mexicans don't care about their fate. Why don't our government officials do anything about it, is the question. We will address that question later in the presentation. We Americans are supposed to be more civilized and advanced than the rest of the world," said Jim.

"You know, these rape trees remind me of the history of Indians and the White people who scalped their enemies. Tying a rape victim's clothing to a tree is like a trophy for these bastards, in the same way that scalping was a trophy," said Bob.

Indians practiced scalping long before the white man arrived. Jacques Cartier, the first European to map the Gulf of Saint Lawrence, met with the Iroquois Indians in 1535. They showed him five scalps that they had taken in their war with the Mohawks. Mohawks were enemies of the Iroquois and they had attacked one of the Iroquois forts, killing 200 inhabitants. In 1564, French artist Jacques Le Moyne witnessed the Timucuan Indians' practice of scalping on the St. Johns River in Florida.

Governor Charles Lawrence of Canada issued a resolution calling for the scalping in 1756 against the Micmac and other Indians. His proclamation said:

"And we do hereby promise, by and with the consent of his Majesty's Council, a reward of thirty pounds for every live male Indian prisoner, above the age of sixteen years, brought in alive; or for a scalp of such male

Indian twenty-five pounds, and twenty-five pounds for every Indian woman or child brought in alive: Such rewards to be paid by the Officer commanding at any of his Majesty's forts in this Provence, immediately upon receiving the Prisoners or Scalps above mentioned, according to the intent and meaning of this Proclamation."

***This proclamation is still on the books. A motion in 2008 to reverse it did not pass. However, the Canadian government says it is not in effect.

"I agree with you, Bob. Rape Trees have been a way for the Mexican traffickers to take a trophy from their victims. These rape trees, with rape victim's underwear attached, are the rapist's trophy. It's a sick and cowardly practice, but that's what we are up against. Many members of these cartels are animals.

"Remember, when you see the reference to young girls, it's about raping children. They must be stopped. Many American government officials, and leading media outlets, have been aware of the extent of the abuse of women and children. They have all turned a 'blind eye' to the crimes. We must identify and expose the government officials and the nation's media as well," said Jim.

"Hey, during World War II, President Franklin Roosevelt and his advisors knew about the concentration camps in Germany and other European countries. They knew that the camps were set up and operating to exterminate Jews, Gypsies, Catholics, homosexuals, political enemies, and many others. Roosevelt did not 'come clean' to the American people about what he and government officials knew and when they knew it," said Bill.

"Not much has changed since the good, old 1930s and 1940s of Roosevelt. Today, our government is not informing the American public about the details of the concentration camps in China. You know—those prisoners that are making athletic shoes and assembling electronics for consumers in the western world.

"Too many members of the Democratic Party in power have self-interests that would be jeopardized if the truth was known about the special deals that many politicians have with the Chinese government. They are just as despicable as the rapists and abusers of the migrant women and children who are trying to make their way to our southern border," said Jim.

The United States government has been covering up, or just ignoring, the truth about the immigration tragedy at the southern border. Top leaders in the administration, the FBI, DOJ, DEA, and Homeland Security have been aware of the abuse of the immigrants for decades.

The current administration has been flying, newly arrived, immigrants to various states in the middle of the night. The immigrants are not vetted and are being sent at night to avoid scrutiny from the American people.

We have a humanitarian crisis, on a grand scale, at the southern border and with few exceptions, American politicians could care less.

We have taken a good look at the history and background of prominent politicians in America. Many of them have been in office for decades and none of them have done anything to protect the American people from the opioid crisis and the crime wave raging in the nation's cities. They are also turning a blind eye to the millions of illegals crossing our southern border and pouring into the United States.

It is easy to criticize the current Administration and Federal Government that comes and goes every four years or so. The real cancer in our society is the many-termed politicians who have done little to protect the American people. They are embedded in both houses of congress.

Let's look at the top nine leaders in the House and Senate. They and their predecessors have determined the fate of the American people over the last eighty years.

These politicians, and their predecessors, are responsible for the terrible conditions that we are witnessing in America today. The opioid crisis, the rampant crime wave that has been raging across the United States for the last three years, and lawlessness. They have allowed the southern border to remain open and uncontrolled since the end of the Trump Administration. It poses the greatest threat to the safety of all Americans.

**Nancy Pelosi** – Former Speaker of the House of Representatives—was born on March 26, 1940 (82). Her father was a Democratic congressman from Maryland. She has not had a job or a responsible position outside of government. Her husband Paul has been employed in the financial sector. His current wealth wasn't realized until Nancy rose in the Democratic Party to take on prominent positions of financial oversight in Congress. Pelosi just finished her eighteenth term in Congress, representing the Twelfth California District, which includes San Francisco. She was first elected to congress in 1987. Sala Burton became ill with cancer and decided not to run in 1988. She picked Pelosi as her designated successor, guaranteeing support from Burton's followers. Burton died in February 1987, a month after being sworn in for another term. Pelosi was able to win the special election to succeed Burton and had been reelected to that office ever since.

**Steny Hamilton Hoyer** – Former House Majority Leader—was born on June 14, 1939 (83). Hoyer is in his twenty-first term in Congress, representing the Fifth District of Maryland. He was first elected to congress in 1981. He has never had employment in the private sector.

**James Enos Clyburn** – Former House Majority Whip—was born on July 21, 1940 (82). Clyburn is in his fifteenth term in Congress, representing the Sixth District of South Carolina. He was a high school teacher in

Charlestown, South Carolina.

**Kevin Owen McCarthy** - Speaker of the House of Representatives—was born on January 26, 1965 (57). McCarthy is in his eighth term in Congress, representing California's Twenty-third District. McCarthy had a short stint working as a small business entrepreneur. He owned his own deli at 19-years of age, while attending college.

**Stephen Joseph Scalise** - House Majority Leader—was born on October 6, 1965 (57). Scalise is in his eighth term in Congress, representing Louisiana's First District, which includes most of New Orleans. Prior to being elected to congress, Scalise served four months in the Louisiana State Senate and three terms in the Louisiana House of Representatives. On June 14, 2017, during practice for the Congressional Baseball Game, Scalise was shot and seriously wounded by a left-wing terrorist and a Bernie Sanders supporter.

**Charles Ellis Schumer** - Senate Majority Leader—was born on November 23, 1950 (71). Schumer is in his fourth Senate term from New York, having held the seat since 1999. Prior to running for the Senate, Schumer served as a three-term member of the New York State Assembly from 1975 to 1980. He served nine terms in the House of Representatives in the Nineth District of New York from 1981 to 1999. Schumer has not held a job outside government.

**Richard Joseph Durkin** - Senate Majority Whip—was born November 21, 1944 (77). Durban is in his fifth Senate term from Illinois, having held the seat since 1997. Prior to joining the Senate, Durbin served seven House terms representing the Twentieth Congressional District. After graduating from law school, he began a legal practice in Springfield, Illinois. He worked as a legal counsel for government agencies prior to running for office.

**Addison Mitchell McConnell** - Senate Minority Leader—was born on February 20,1942 (80). McConnell is in his seventh Senate term from Kentucky, having held the seat since 1985. Outside of government employment, McConnell spent a few years as a member of a law firm in Louisville.

**John Randolph Thune** - Senate Minority Whip—was born on January 7, 1961 (61). Thune is in his third Senate term from South Dakota, having served since 2004. Prior to joining the Senate, he was a three-term congressman representing South Dakota's at-large Congressional District from 1997 to 2003.

Many of these politicians have become wealthy while holding government office. Somehow, they have become rich while receiving a modest government income. It is easy to trace their records of newfound wealth.

While they have been in office representing the people, some of them have been quite blatant in their behavior. They have shown no fear in obtaining illicit wealth. Many of them have been involved in insider-trading. They have been steering their investment counselors, or relatives, to companies receiving contracts from the government. (Contracts that their House or Senate committees have oversight of for the benefit and protection of the American people.)

Their investment counselors, or friends and relatives, purchase company stock at just the right time in order to receive a windfall stock value. It's a rigged and corrupt system. Congressional members are hesitant to investigate their colleagues for corruption. Therefore, the corrupt continue to prosper from year to year and the system rewards the wrong doer.

While these politicians have been in office, and have taken an oath to the Constitution with a mandate to protect the American people, the following has taken place:

- American cities have been turned into "killing fields"—hundreds of drug overdoses and shootings occur every week.
- City streets in San Francisco, L.A. and other cities are littered with human feces and discarded drug needles.
- Women and the elderly are assaulted and beaten on the

streets in broad daylight by the homeless and habitual criminals—sometimes losing their lives. In cities like New York, elderly Asian people have been special targets of the homeless and mentally ill criminals.

- Tent Cities, inhabited by the homeless, have created significant health-hazards. They have taken over public property in many communities and the inhabitants threaten the safety of the public.

- In the last two years, over 100,000 people in America, between the ages of twenty-one and forty-five, have died from fentanyl overdoses. Huge quantities of the deadly fentanyl drug have been trafficked by drug cartel couriers across the wide-open southern border and into the United States.

- Congressional leaders, from both parties', have been pre-occupied with jockeying for political power. The climate change hysteria, war in Ukraine, and China's efforts to harass the people of Taiwan have left them ignoring the crisis at the southern border. This is a greater threat to the well-being and safety of the American people.

"So, Jim. What are your plans? How are you and the Source going to go after these people and problems?" asked Don.

"Suffice it to say, we have a multi-pronged attack plan to stop the coyotes, the illegal drug production, and the cartel money laundering operations. Our plan will separate the coyotes from the immigrants, destroy the drug processing plants, and separate the cartel leaders from their cash. I'll go into detail in our afternoon session," said Jim.

# CHAPTER EIGHT

# THE EMISSARIES

Jim sent his three emissaries to Austin, Texas, to meet with state government officials. Their mission was to inform the officials about Jim's and the Source's recent actions against the cartels.

They were Jim's closest childhood friends, and he prepared them to give individual presentations, on his behalf, to the officials and a few of the largest ranch-owners.

Robert (Bob) Dixon's, William (Bill) Andrew's, and Donald (Don) Ferenz's plane landed at the Austin-Bergstrom International Airport. They were greeted by two government officials in a limousine and were whisked away to the Austin Marriott Hotel in downtown Austin. When they checked into their rooms, a hotel clerk informed them of the location of the conference room. It had been reserved for their scheduled meeting at 9 am the following morning.

Bob Dixon had been a very successful salesman in Silicon Valley, California for over thirty years. He had sold printed circuit boards manufactured in Taiwan and electronic components manufactured in Japan by Japanese conglomerates. His suppliers could supply the key components for all computers and workstations designed by high-tech companies in Silicon Valley. His retirement from sales was timely as the dominance of hardware technology shifted to software solutions. Emerging software had incorporated much of the technology that had been provided by hardware components.

Bob did not want to put forth the effort to become knowledgeable about software. It was a good time to leave.

Prior to his employment in Silicon Valley, Bob had served in the Army and had been stationed in Germany. His unit had the mission of guarding the West German/East German border. Most of his duty assignments were with the color guard, and he regularly performed at military ceremonies or marched in parades.

Now retired, Bob had gray hair with a receding hair line. He was in his early seventies and was portly in stature. His three children were grown, had left home, and were pursuing their own careers. His wife, Marci, was busy with her friends, shopping or working almost daily with two local charities. He didn't care to play golf, and he didn't have any hobbies. With little to do after his retirement, he soon became bored. He looked forward to the adventures that were offered to him by his close friend, Jim. He was also fascinated, and a little intimidated, by the extra-terrestrials working with Jim. He was still mystified over why they had chosen to work with Jim.

Don Ferenz had had a twenty-five-year career in education. First, as a high school math teacher and later as a superintendent of schools. He was not eligible for the draft due to a congenital heart valve problem. With his medical issues, he was able to avoid the military. He had been eager to spend a career teaching, but after ten years was burned out with the politics in education. He was contemplating a new career.

Don's work as a school superintendent also turned out to be disappointing due to the politics that went along with the job. He had stayed for an additional fifteen years until he had finally had enough. He chose to retire before doing something that he would regret, to his "asshole" supervisor.

While teaching, he had studied real estate and was able to obtain his real estate license. He was moderately successful in his new career selling real estate, but after ten years in the business, he was ready to completely retire. In his retirement he had hired a personal trainer and they had developed a daily exercise regimen to counter his weight gain and to get in better shape. Always stocky in frame, Don was naturally strong, and enjoyed seeing the development of his muscular build. He was thrilled to see a rapid weight loss and was disappointed that he hadn't started a workout program years before.

His children were grown, and his wife was busy with her friends and numerous activities. He was looking for something stimulating to counter his daily boredom.

When his childhood friend, Jim, offered him an opportunity to get involved in a crazy scheme involving visiting former president Trump's compound in Florida, he was energized. He didn't quite buy into Jim's story about working with extraterrestrials, but he didn't really care. He wanted something exciting to do. He avoided saying anything to his wife about the UFOs and extraterrestrials, and she wasn't interested enough to ask. While working with Jim, he had never seen an extraterrestrial, but he had seen the damage that had been done to the FBI vehicles and equipment.

Now, Jim was calling about a new mission and he was excited.

William (Bill) Andrew had joined the Marines during the Vietnam War. He was looking for an adventure. After advanced training, the Marines responded to his enthusiasm by sending him to I-Corps in Vietnam. His unit fought some of the bloodiest battles of the war. He witnessed a lot of dying and lost four of his good friends. When it was his time to rotate out of Vietnam, he was ready. He loved the Marine Corps, but he had lost his enthusiasm for war. Upon being discharged, the VA had diagnosed him to be suffering from post-traumatic stress disorder (PTSD). He would carry the mental disorder with him for the rest of his life.

Bill was a handsome man who had always loved the ladies. He made friends easily and had a personality that allowed him to get away with saying controversial things. After being discharged from the military, he attended college. He went to work for government contractors who made military equipment. He became an expert on drone technology. With his children grown and on their own, and being retired, he had nothing to do. His wife, Thelma, continued to work as a nurse at a local medical clinic and he was home alone, looking for the next step in his life. He enjoyed cooking and made great meals for Thelma and himself, but as much as he loved cooking, he didn't think that he was good enough to make a living as a chef. When his childhood friend Jim called him again with a new mission, he was thrilled.

# CHAPTER NINE

# GONE TO TEXAS

Jim chose Texas as the first state to send his emissaries. It was the largest American portal where illegal immigrants and heavy drug trafficking entered unabated. Jim wanted his emissaries to explain his, and the Source's, actions against the drug cartels. He wanted an audience of conservative Americans who might be interested in collaborating with him in the future.

Don Ferenz, Bill Andrew, and Bob Dixon met in Dallas, Texas with state government officials and five of the most prominent ranchers. Each friend had the responsibility of explaining a third of Jim's presentation regarding his and the Source's attack on drug cartels, the illegal flow of China-based fentanyl, and other drugs.

Don had the responsibility of presenting the strategy of attack on the cartels' huge drug caches of cash. The cash was in warehouses in Mexico City and waiting to be shipped to Hong Kong.

Bill had the task of explaining how Jim and the Source were intercepting and preventing the current flow of illegal and deadly fentanyl from Chinese-controlled drug labs. Chinese operatives had been shipping fentanyl and drug adulterants to Mexico to be integrated by the cartels with their cocaine and heroin. The deadly "drug cocktail" was then smuggled across the United States' southern border for consumption by Americans.

Bob's role was to explain how Jim and the Source were destroying the drug processing plants in Mexico and in Central American countries. He also provided a detailed explanation of the Source's assault on the "human coyotes" who were luring, guiding, and abusing vulnerable migrants. The migrants had been walking and riding in caravans towards the southern border of the United States. They were hoping to be accepted by the government and the American people.

The meeting attendees included three officials from the Governor's office. The Texas Rangers had sent four of their top officers. Five ranch-owners, with a combined ownership of over two million acres of land had been invited by the Governor's office as they were very powerful and influential in Texas politics.

The Texas Rangers is an investigative law enforcement agency with statewide jurisdiction in the state of Texas. Its headquarters are in Austin, Texas. There are 166 commissioned members on the Ranger force. The Rangers are culturally significant to Texans and are legally protected against disbandment.

The Texas audience was very enthusiastic and happy to meet with the three representatives and learn firsthand about Jim's and the Source's activities. They were fascinated to learn about the involvement with the extraterrestrials. The Texans wanted to know how they could participate in the work that Jim and the Source were doing. They wanted to work with Jim against the cartels and the drug epidemic.

Don was the first presenter to speak. His presentation focused on the attack strategies that Jim and the Source were employing against the drug cartels and the massive amounts of cash stored in cartel-owned warehouses in Mexico City.

Don began his presentation, "The leading Mexican cartels are Sinaloa, La Familia, Knights Templar, and the Juarez Cartel.

"One of the major problems that the drug cartels were confronted with was what to do with the huge amounts of cash that had been generated by their sales of illegal drugs. Their biggest challenge was to find ways to convert drug money into usable currency.

"The leaders of the drug cartels might be uneducated and crude in their behavior, but many of them are capable, deceitful, strategists and sophisticated businessmen. Their operations are dependent on their ability to identify loopholes in legal and financial systems. They hire the best and most talented people to pursue their goals. They pay them extremely well in order to secure and maintain their loyalty and participation.

"Cartels had hired teams of computer specialists to hack into data networks, global banking systems, government agencies, and they also monitored law enforcement communications.

"In the past, cartels had used every method possible to launder their illegal cash. They had tried to use financial institutions to deposit their money. One method, called layering, utilized wire transfers to different accounts, with different names, under the guise of purchasing imported commodities. These methods were too cumbersome though to deal with the accelerating amounts of cash. The IRS required banks to report any deposits over $10,000. That was too small an amount to have any positive impact on cartel cash holdings," said Don.

(In 2012, Europe's largest bank, HSBC, was caught providing money laundering services of more than $881 million in narcotics profits for the Mexican cartel, Sinaloa, and Columbia's Norte del Valle cartel. HSBC agreed to pay a $1.9 billion penalty due to a "lack of adequate control processes in compliance and anti-money laundering.")

Don continued with his presentation, "In 2020, an article in Reuters reported that Chinese 'money brokers' had emerged as vital partners for Latin American drug cartels. They were becoming key cogs in their multi-billion-dollar empires and upending the way narcotics cash traditionally had been laundered, according to U.S. authorities.

"The article continued to explain that a popular method that Chinese brokers employed to launder U.S. drug proceeds of Mexican crime groups was the following:

**Step 1**

A Mexican cartel wants to bring proceeds from U.S. drug sales back to Mexico. It contacts Chinese money-brokers operating in Mexico to see who offers the cheapest rates.

**Step 2**

The parties agree on a commission and the amount to be laundered, as an example—$150,000.

**Step 3**

The Chinese broker, using encrypted phone messages, would send the cartel three things:

A code word

The number of a U.S. burner phone

The unique serial number of an authentic USD

**Step 4**

The Mexican crime group shares those details with a cartel-linked drug dealer in the United States, who calls the burner phone and identifies himself using the code word. He arranges to meet a U.S.-based money courier working for the Chinese broker.

**Step 5**

The drug dealer and the money courier meet in public. The courier hands over the cash, keeping the bill as a 'receipt.'

**Step 6**

The courier takes the USD $150,000 to a U.S.-based Chinese merchant who has a bank account in China. The merchant then performs a currency swap know as a 'mirror transaction.' He takes possession of the U.S. cash and then transfers USD $150,000 worth of Chinese yuan from his Chinese bank account to the money-broker's Chinese account, using an account number provided to him by the courier.

**Step 7**

The Cartel's drug cash is now sitting in a Chinese bank, outside the view of U.S. law enforcement. The broker now has two options to send it on to Mexico to the drug cartel.

**Step 8**

Option 1 is to do another 'mirror transaction.' The USD $150,000 worth of yuan is now transferred from the money-broker's Chinese account to a Mexico-based businessperson's Chinese bank account. That Mexico-based businessperson then provides USD $150,000 worth of pesos to the money-broker in Mexico, who delivers the cash to the cartel.

**Step 9**

Under option 2, the Chinese money-broker buys USD $150,000 worth of consumer products in China, such as clothing, and exports them to Mexico. The goods are then sold, and the proceeds are delivered to the cartel," explained Don.

**(In June 2020, a Chinese national pleaded guilty in the United States to conspiracy to commit money-laundering after laundering more than $4 million USD for Mexican cartels.)**

"It is well understood in the global business world, that Chinese nationals must have permission, support, and involvement of the Chinese Communist Party (CCP) to operate businesses or be part of any financial transactions, whether they be legal or illegal," said Don.

"Jim Vincent and the Source had been executing a plan to disrupt and destroy a more ominous money-laundering scheme that had been instituted by the Chinese government and the Mexican cartels.

"The small transactions that had been conducted in the past were ineffective and too cumbersome. They were acceptable to use when dealing in hundreds and thousands of dollars in cash. They were not practical when dealing with cash amounts approaching hundreds of millions or billions of dollars.

"The Chinese and the Mexican cartels had decided to take a chapter out of the Obama-Biden administration's 'surreptitious playbook.'

"Obama's administration had flown pallets of cash, amounting to almost $2 billion, to the Iranians in the middle of the night.

"With the infusion of the illegal fentanyl transactions that had significantly increased the amount of cash, the CCP had decided to accept planeloads of Mexican cartel cash to be flown directly from Mexico City into Hong Kong. The cash had been designated to be laundered through Hong Kong banks and other banks controlled by the CCP," said Don.

On January 17, 2016, the day following the release of four Americans detained by the Iranians, a jumbo jet carrying $400 million in euros, Swiss francs, and other currencies landed in Tehran. The money allegedly was a partial payment of a claim by Iran for U.S. military equipment that was never delivered. Soon after, $1.3 billion in cash was flown into Tehran by the United States government.

The payment to the Iranians was taken from the Treasury Department's Judgement Fund.

The Obama-Biden administration finally admitted to the American people, in September 2016, that the payment to the Iranians had been in cash.

Don continued, "The CCP controls and monitors all banking transactions in Hong Kong. They had directed the banks to launder the cartel cash and deposit the cartel's share in Hong Kong bank accounts in the names that were designated by the cartels. The CCP had negotiated the cost of the money-laundering with the cartels. Very significant shares of the cash had been deposited in the bank accounts of members of the CCP."

"Jim Vincent and the Source had been interdicting the illegal cash flow of the cartels, using their advanced technology. The Source had 'obliterated' pallets of drug money in cartel-owned warehouses in Mexico City. CCP leaders were enraged, due to their fentanyl shipments being interrupted by the loss of the cartel cash. The Mexican cartels were running out of cash to execute the fentanyl transactions with the Chinese government," said Don.

"How do Jim and the Source locate the cartels' cash in the warehouses?" asked John Slaughter of the Texas Rangers.

"They track the cash shipments from each cartel's headquarters to the warehouses in Mexico City. The drugs are packaged on pallets, designated to be flown to Hong Kong," said Don.

"How are they able to destroy the cash being stored on the pallets?" asked Susan Swann of the Governor's office.

"The Source has advanced technology that the United States doesn't possess. It resembles our laser technology in a minor way. They can burnup the cash while not doing damage to anything around the pallets. Their 'laser-like' technology doesn't destroy the warehouses either," replied Don.

"How much cash has been destroyed?" asked John Roberts of the Governor's office.

"We don't know the total amount, but we believe that they have destroyed hundreds of millions of dollars. Enough has been destroyed for the cartels and their Mexican government stooges to be at each other's throats, looking for who to hold responsible," said Don.

"This is great. What else are you doing to stop the cartels and the Chinese?" asked ranch owner Harold Clements.

"As I mentioned at the start of my presentation, I'm only providing a third of Jim Vincent's plan. Tomorrow morning, Bill Andrew will discuss the drug flow and later, Bob Dixon will cover the destruction of the drug processing plants and fentanyl labs. Let's break for now and go to dinner," suggested Don.

# CHAPTER TEN

# THE GLOBAL DRUG EPIDEMIC

The following morning, Bill Andrew began the second part of Jim Vincent's presentation. His part focused on the global drug epidemic and the methods used by Jim and the Source to intercept the deadly flow of drugs.

Bill began, "The Chinese Communist Party (CCP) was founded by Li Dazhao, Chen Du, and others in 1921 as a political party and revolutionary movement. In 1949, after the Nationalists had been decisively defeated and had retreated to Taiwan, the CCP founded the People's Republic of China.

"At first, the CCP adopted the Soviet model for development and aligned itself with the Soviet Union. By the end of the 1950s, the CCP and the Soviet Union had broken their ties with each other."

In the late 1950s and early 1960s, the CCP developed innovated programs, such as the Great Leap Forward (1958–1962) to hasten China's industrial development. The programs turned out to be harmful, with disastrous results. They created widespread famine. It was the deadliest famine and one of the greatest "man-made" disasters in human history. There was an estimated death toll of approximately thirty-eight million people. It was determined that the famine had been the result of an insufficient distribution of food, poor agricultural techniques, over reporting of grain production and ordering millions of farmers to switch to iron and steel production.

During this period, Mao Zedong (1893–1976), founder of the People's Republic of China, sent seven million tons of grain to the Soviet Union along with tons of meat, cooking oil, eggs, and other foodstuffs. This was in exchange for Soviet military weapons and technology to create the "bomb."

**If all this food had not been exported, and had instead been distributed to the masses, not a single person in China would have died from hunger.**

Mao saw practical advantages in massive deaths. "Deaths have benefits," he told the top echelon of the CCP, on December 9, 1958. "They can fertilize the ground."

The Chinese government ordered peasants to plant crops over burial plots. This caused intense anguish among the Chinese people.

## The Chinese Politburo

The Politburo of the Chinese Communist Party (CCP) is the decision-making body of the party. The Standing Committee of the CCP is a committee consisting of the top leadership. It is composed of seven members, including Xi Jinping, General Secretary of the CCP and President of the People's Republic of China.

The current twenty-five members of the Politburo were born, raised and educated, during Mao Zedong's brutal control over the Chinese people. Almost all of them were in their mid-twenties when Mao died in 1976.

## Mao Zedong

During his reign, Mao had been responsible for the deaths, from starvation and murder, of approximately 71 million Chinese people. Mao advocated strict Communist Party control and his Party, led by the current Politburo, maintains an iron grip over political power and all aspects of life.

## Xi Jinping

Today, Xi and the members of China's Politburo, are more sophisticated and educated than were Mao and his contemporaries. Still, their beliefs and methods are equally as cruel and brutal as the Maoists.

Currently, China is leading and empowering the global drug epidemic for the purpose of weakening and eventually obtaining dominance over the

West. They are financing the Mexican drug cartels by laundering their mountains of drug cash. In exchange for the laundering of the cash, they supply the cartels with deadly fentanyl and drug adulterants from their labs in China. The Chinese-based fentanyl has been colored in "Easter-candy colors" to entice the young and innocent, as well as increase demand.

China's long-term goal is world dominance. The Chinese will resort to any method to gain world dominance—launder drug money for the cartels, murder their own citizens who defy them, assassinate enemies, and poison Americans with fentanyl disguised as candy.

"Our government must be aware of China's role in the global drug epidemic. What are we doing to curb China's harming the United States? What are we doing to protect our country?" asked Thomas Wood of the Texas Rangers.

"The Administration is going easy on China and acting timid. It could be that the Chinese have a covert influence on the Administration's decision-makers. China has a growing list of former American politicians on its payroll, lobbying on their behalf and against the best interests of the American people. They certainly have had Biden family-members in their pocket," said Bill.

The current members of the CCP are strongly influenced by the teachings of Mao. All of them grew up during his reign of terror. They are as ruthless as Mao, and they are capable of the same insane programs that Mao perpetuated.

When Mao was in Moscow in 1957, he had said, "We are prepared to sacrifice 300 million Chinese for the victory of the world revolution."

That was about half the population of China at that time.

In 1964, Mao ordered a massive relocation of his arms-centered industries. Mao said that this was "house moving" of industries to cope with the "Era of the Bomb." This undertaking went by the general name of "The Third Front." More than 1,100 large enterprises were dismantled and moved to remote areas where major installations, like steel and electricity plants, had to be reconstructed. Some nuclear facilities were even duplicated.

For up to two decades, families were torn apart. Over four million people were forced to build factories in the mountains, lay railways, and open mines. They worked and lived in appalling conditions.

Many died.

In private, Mao composed two lines of doggerel:
"Atom bomb goes off when it is told.
Ah, what boundless joy!"
Source: Jung Chang

"China must be stopped now before it is too late," said Bill.

# THE DEATH OF INNOCENTS

Jane Miller, Sonya Thompson, and Marcella Fernandez were eighteen years old and recent graduates of Saint Mary's High School in San Jose, California. They were very attractive, athletic young women. They had been close friends since grammar school. They were exceptional soccer players, and they each had received recruitment letters from many colleges.

Jane chose to play soccer at San Jose State and Sonya chose the University of California, at Berkeley. Marcella had chosen to play at the University of Texas, in Austin. She had many relatives in Texas, and they had encouraged her to choose Austin.

The three planned to celebrate with friends at Don's Grill, a popular restaurant in downtown San Jose, before leaving for their respective colleges.

Don's Grill was located a few blocks from San Jose State. It was a popular sports bar and hangout, frequented by students, athletes, and fraternity members.

The three women-athletes had been drinking beer and talking loudly with friends. Jane and Sonya suddenly slumped down in their chairs. They whispered to friends that they couldn't breathe. Marcella had put her head in her arms on the table. Her friends thought that she had fallen asleep.

When two Emergency Medical Service officers (EMS) arrived, they were unable to revive Marcella. She was dead. They worked feverously to revive Jane and Sonya. An EMS asked Sonya what they had taken. She could barely speak, but she was able to moan that her friend Tim had given them some colored pills when they had arrived at the bar. Tim had said the pills would give them a safe high.

The EMS team was unable to determine what drug the women had ingested.

Jane and Sonya died in the ambulance on the way to the hospital. It wouldn't have mattered if the EMS team had discovered that the drug was fentanyl. They didn't have the drug, Narcan, with them when they responded to the emergency. Later, they would carry Narcan with them on all emergency calls.

Naloxone, known to the public as Narcan, is an opioid-reversal agent. It works by rapidly binding to opioid receptors and blocking the effects of opioid drugs. Fentanyl is stronger than other opioid drugs, such as morphine, and might require multiple doses of naloxone.

The police investigation identified Tim Brown as the individual who had given the women the pills and they arrested him.

Tim Brown was twenty-two-years-old. His father was African American, and his mother was of Irish and Scottish descent. His father was a rabid fan of the Oakland Raiders football team. He had named his son, Tim, after the Raiders' Hall of Famer, Tim Brown.

Tim had been an exceptional athlete in high school as a running back on the football team. He was severely injured in a game during his senior year. He received a head injury that resulted in the left side of his body being paralyzed for two days. He had been traumatized by the temporary paralysis. When he recovered, he vowed that he would never risk his life playing a contact sport.

Tim drifted after high school. He attended San Jose State as a communication major but was never a serious student. His poor grades did not allow him to stay in college. He had been popular in school—always smiling and telling jokes. He could sing and decided to try Rap. He adopted the Rap name, "Rhoda-Roota."

When Tim was hired as a DJ for his cousin's wedding, he added rap music to his performance. He was warmly received by the wedding guests.

He decided to include his rapping with all his DJ performances.

As his popularity grew, the new up-and-coming Rapper/DJ, Tim, began to sell drugs to supplement his income. At every party that he worked; he observed that the partygoers were doing drugs. He began to make more money selling drugs than performing as a DJ. He started to use his DJ jobs as an in-road to be selling more drugs.

Tim was a good friend of Sonya Thompsons' older brother, Jason. He and Jason had played football together. They had even double-dated to the high school prom.

When he ran into Sonya at one of his DJ gigs, she asked him if he would score some drugs for her and her friends. "We want something safe, Tim. It's just to celebrate our graduation," Sonya explained to him.

"Sonya. I don't like doing this. Jason is my best friend," said Tim. Sonya continued with her request, saying it was a onetime request. Tim relented and handed her three pills. The pills were brightly colored and looked like candy.

"You will each only need one. They will get you guys high enough to have a good time. Don't ever ask me for drugs again, Sonya. You and Jason are like family to me. Jason better not find out that you got these from me either," said Tim.

"Thank you, Tim. Just this one time. I won't ever ask you again," said Sonya.

The police investigation could not prove that Tim had given the fentanyl pills to the three women. He was released the next day. He would never emotionally recover from the realization that he had been responsible for the deaths of the three women.

Tim left California and moved to New Orleans to live with an aunt and uncle.

# CHAPTER TWELVE

# HUMAN COYOTES

"My presentation this morning will focus on the human trafficking from Mexico and Central America, the destruction of drug processing plants, and Chinese fentanyl labs by Jim and the Source," said Bob Dixon.

**Coyote: A person who smuggles immigrants, especially Latin Americans, into the United States for a high fee.**

The most successful strategy of the Mexican drug cartels has been to organize, control, and guide human trafficking (Coyotes), in caravans of migrants from Central America and Mexico. The thousands of migrants approaching the United States southern border occupy the daily activities and drain the resources of the American border patrol. While guiding the migrants into the arms of the border patrol, the cartels avoid the authorities and can ship their drugs through other areas of the border not manned by U.S. government agents.

Bob continued, "I'd like to begin by highlighting a very tragic story of the murder of innocent migrants by Mexican human-smugglers.

"On the evening of June 27, 2022, authorities in San Antonio, Texas, were alerted by an emergency-911 call. It concerned a stopped tractor-trailer. A passerby was flagged down for help by a migrant who had escaped from the truck. The tractor-trailer may have been carrying as many as 100 migrants, but the exact number was unclear.

"Authorities speculated that the truck had had mechanical problems and had been left parked next to railroad tracks. Temperatures had reached 103 degrees Fahrenheit. There were no signs of water or air-conditioning inside the truck.

"When authorities approached the truck, they quickly observed a horrific scene. They found the back door open with 'stacks of bodies' inside. Other bodies had collapsed nearby. Some of the dead victims' bodies were 'hot to the touch.'

"Officials said, 'The victims' bodies had been sprinkled with a pungent substance.' It is a practice that some human smugglers use to mask the scent of human cargo and evade canine detection.

"Most of the deceased migrants, thirty-nine men and twelve women, were from Mexico. Seven of the dead were from Guatemala and two victims were from Honduras.

"According to U.S. Representative Henry Cuellar, 'The driver of the truck and two other people were arrested.'

"The authorities had traced the tractor-trailer's registration to a San Antonio address that had been under surveillance. Two Mexican citizens,

Juan Francisco D'Luna-Bilbao and Juan Claudio D'Luna-Mendez were arrested as they were leaving the residence. They were also charged with possessing firearms while residing in the United States illegally.

"A third suspect, Homero Zamorano, forty-five, driver of the truck, was described as an American citizen. He had been taken into custody, was very high on meth, and had to be transported to a hospital immediately.

"The tragedy marked the greatest loss of life on record from human trafficking, according to a special agent with the U.S. Immigration and Customs Enforcement (ICE)," said Bob.

"Where is the FBI in all of this?" asked John Slaughter of the Texas Rangers.

"Nowhere. They seem to be more interested in pursuing enemies of the Democratic Party. Their top leadership is corrupt and politicized," replied Bob.

The incident in San Antonio, on June 27, 2022, was not the first event involving the deaths and suffering of migrants in tractor-trailers.

In 2013, nineteen migrants were found sweltering in a truck in southwest San Antonio.

In 2017, ten migrants had died from being trapped in a truck at a San Antonio Walmart. The driver was later sentenced to life in prison for his role in the smuggling operation.

In 2018, fifty migrants were found alive in a truck driven by a man who was paid $3,000 to drive the truck—he was sentenced to five years in prison.

Multiple sources, including *The Guardian* and the *Associated Press*, reported in July 2021, "Forty-three bodies found in Arizona borderland amid brutal heat".

Humane Borders is a 501c3 humanitarian organization headquartered in Tucson, Arizona. They reported that the remains of the forty-three migrants were found on the border in June, which was the hottest month on-record in Phoenix. Temperatures are regularly above 110 Fahrenheit. The organization maps the recovery of bodies in Arizona using data from a medical examiner's office in Tucson. The leading cause of death is exposure. The group's figures include all bodies that are recovered and believed to have been migrants. Humane Borders numbers are higher than the number of deaths reported by the border patrol who only count those they handle in the course of their work.

Humane Borders, and other humanitarian organizations like Tucson Samaritans and No More Deaths, leave water jugs and supplies in remote parts of the desert in hopes of saving dehydrated migrants. More than 3,700 migrant deaths have been documented in the region. Smuggling organizations are abandoning migrants in remote and dangerous areas.

"What's the Mexican government doing on their side to stop the flow of immigrants?" asked Bill Evans, a local rancher.

"With Trump no longer in the White House, the Mexicans have withdrawn their troops from the border, and they do nothing to stop the flow of immigrants," said Bob.

"The following are some additional data points that reflect the true condition on the southern border," said Bob.

United States Customs and Border protection (CBP) encountered 1,662,167 migrants in fiscal 2021—that number jumped to nearly two million when counting those who were immediately turned away at the border. Most people encountered at the border were expelled under the Title 42 authority. This was to prevent the spread of coronavirus disease (Covid-19). The CBP blamed the massive spike in border crossing on multiple factors.

In September 2021, more than 36,000 migrants from Ecuador were caught by the U.S. Border Patrol Agents compared with 35,066 Mexican nationals. The Mexican nationals historically top the list of those who try to illegally cross the border into the United States. Ecuadorians typically pay up to $15,000 per person to human smugglers to reach the American southern border.

- In November 2021, crossers included 63,000 Mexican citizens, and 50,000 people from the Northern Triangle countries of El Salvador, Guatemala, and Honduras. Another 61,000 people arrived from other nations.

- The going rate paid to smugglers for Central Americans trying to reach the United States ranges from $8,000 to $12,000. According to the United States Customs and Border Patrol Protection public affairs officer, Landon Hutchens, the further you go into South America, the price that the transnational criminal organizations charge increases from $12,000 to $15,000 per person.

- The human smugglers (coyotes), promise comfortable rides in air-conditioned buses and lodging in clean hotels.
- According to Border Patrol Agents, the coyotes also tell the

migrants that the Administration is giving "free amnesty." The coyotes often lie to the migrants, some of them traveling from as far away as Haiti and Turkey, about the distance they will have to travel when they are left at the frontier between Mexico and the United States.

- Some coyotes have abandoned children, as young as three-years-old, in scorching scrubland where rattlesnakes and animal coyotes roam.

- Most smugglers are affiliated with the Sinaloa and La Linea drug cartels, based in Ciudad Juarez.

- In April 2021, Border Patrol agents rescued an eight-year-old boy abandoned in New Mexico, "walking aimlessly through the desert by himself," according to a Border Patrol report.

- On July 1, 2021, according to El Paso Sector Border Patrol Agents, coyotes abandoned five unaccompanied children from Guatemala near the Ysleta port of entry in southeastern El Paso. The children, ages fourteen to seventeen, became stranded in the rushing waters of the Rio Grande. They were in danger of drowning before they were pulled out of the water by the agents.

- A national security problem for the American people is the number of "Got-Aways," illegal immigrants, who have been able to avoid apprehension from Border Patrol agents. The number has reached an historic high and is an ongoing crisis at the United States – Mexico border. Data from a Freedom of Information Act request shows that shortly after Joe Biden became president in January 2020, the number of estimated "Got-Aways" skyrocketed nationwide.

- Mark Morgan, acting commissioner of CBP, said the 'Got-Aways' will number around 600,000 by the end of the year—and that's even low. There are many 'Got-Aways' that they haven't been able to count."

- The inability for the Border Patrol to count "Got-Aways" is due to the many agents who are being assigned to the processing of thousands of illegal immigrants. The immigrants are willingly turning themselves in. The agents must also transport the large groups from the border to the holding facilities.

- Townhall Media received leaked documents showing that many work shifts in the Yuma Sector did not have agents assigned to tracking the "Got-Aways." Even when they did, it was only one assigned agent.

A letter sent to the Biden administration, and signed by 275 sheriffs from thirty-nine states, warned the President of dangerous repercussions if he continued to allow illegal immigrants to flow, unchecked, into the country.

The letter read:

**America's Sheriffs are deeply troubled about the dangerous impacts your administration's border policies are having on our citizens, legal residents, and communities.**

**You must act now before our nation's public safety resources are overwhelmed with the criminal side effects of unchecked illegal immigration, including transnational gangs, guns, dangerous drugs, and human trafficking.**

**As this situation continues to evolve, more families will be exposed to the violence associated with drug trafficking and transnational gangs. More parents will suffer the loss of their children, because of exposure to criminal illegal alien violence caused by the reckless and irresponsible policies of your administration.**

**In a myriad of ways, you and your administration are encouraging and sanctioning lawlessness and the victimization of the people of the United States of America, all in the name of mass illegal immigration.**

**In the interests of ending the undermining of our laws and the increased risks to the safety and security of the people of the United States of America, we respectfully request that you immediately reverse course on your pro-illegal immigration policies, resume the border wall construction, and embrace the common-sense, public-safety-supporting border policies of the previous administration."**

Bob continued, "The Biden administration has refused to call the situation at the border a crisis, but the border numbers are making the administration's refusal difficult to uphold. Unaccompanied children have proven especially difficult for the President. In March 2022, Border Agents had encountered over 19,000 children at the border—the largest number ever recorded in a single month."

Bob went on to explain. "Jim and the Source determined that the most effective way to stop the massive flow of illegal drugs was to stop the caravans of immigrants being used as decoys by the cartels in making their drug shipments.

"At the same time, they reasoned that if the drug processing plants were destroyed at the Source of the drug manufacturing, the cartels' supply chain would be 'squeezed,' and they would be unable to continue their illegal operations.

"They targeted the human-smugglers known as 'coyotes' who recruited, abused, and guided the thousands of immigrants towards the United States southern border.

"When Jim and the Source observed coyotes, organizing groups of immigrants, the Source burned holes in the smugglers' feet. Seeing the coyotes being attacked, the immigrants were horrified and afraid for their lives. They fled from the caravan staging areas.

"The Source attacked the human-smugglers from the Central American countries where the immigrants had begun their journey through Mexico. Those who already had crossed the border into the United States, were also attacked. The smugglers had holes burned through their feet and they were unable to walk.

"The Source also attacked the cartels' drug processing plants in Guatemala, El Salvador, Honduras and Mexico. The Source destroyed the plants without harming plant workers," said Bob.

"Have the caravans stopped? Have the cartels' processing plants really been destroyed?" asked John Slaughter of the Texas Rangers.

"Yes. Most everything has been stopped. There's no guarantee that the cartels will not start up again, but their operations are crippled for now," said Bob.

"Then what is left for us to do?" asked Slaughter.

"You can take back the city streets and territory that was relinquished to the cartels. You can get tough on crime and hold criminals accountable. You can give the American people a sense of security that they lost to the cartels and criminals," said Bob.

"What's the next step?" asked a member from the Governor's office.

Bob responded, "Jim and the Source have no faith that the Administration or any of its federal agencies will protect the American people from the invasion at the southern border.

"They want everyone here to be informed of what they are doing to protect against the attacks by the cartels and the Chinese drug channel.

"Hopefully, the state of Texas, its law enforcement agencies, and you ranchers are willing to collaborate with them."

"We certainly are ready to work with them. We'll get everyone here in Texas to take back our cities and land from these bastards. We'll go after the federal government and its 'do-nothing' agencies. You tell Jim and the Source that we are with them and that we want to start right away," said Thomas Johnson, a ranch owner.

After the last meeting concluded, Tom Johnson announced to Jim's three emissaries that he had a treat for them. He wanted to show his appreciation for their visit to Texas.

"Fellas. Y'all are going on a little cattle drive tomorra for a few hours. Then we're going to finish up with a real Texas barbecue as a thank you for y'all coming down here to help Texas.

"Are you kidding me? I've never been on a horse," Don whispered to Bill and Bob.

"Donny. Don't worry. You'll be the first 'Portuguese Cowboy' to ride the range in Texas. You'll be famous. They might even put up a statue in your honor," said Bob.

"What if they give me a wild one? I knew I should have bought more life insurance before I came down here," said Don.

"I'm not particularly fond of horses myself. I was bucked off one when I was ten. I tried to ride our neighbor's horse," said Bill.

"What did your neighbor do? Didn't they try to teach you how to ride?" asked Don.

"It wasn't like that," said Bill. They didn't know that a couple of us kids had snuck into the barn and put a saddle on their horse. It was an old horse and very calm. I think it was about twenty-two-years old—ready to die. When we led it out of the barn, I got on him. He immediately threw me off and the saddle landed on top of me. I hit the ground hard. The old horse just stood there and looked at me. So, we led him back into the barn and gave him some hay."

The three emissaries, Don, Bob, and Bill, had had a challenging time on the cattle drive. When Bob finished up and turned in his horse, he complained that his hemorrhoids had hemorrhoids.

Bill's horse had stopped suddenly as it approached a small creek. He flew over the horse's head into the water. His clothes were soaked, and the inside of his legs were chafed from his wet pants rubbing against the saddle. The last hour of the ride had been miserable.

Don had been nervous during the entire ride, even though they gave him the meekest horse. When he crossed the small creek, he fell forward in his saddle and hugged his horse's neck to keep from falling into the water.

He was holding on for dear life when one of the professional cowboys guiding the drive rode up to him and said, "Ease up there, buddy. Stay calm and let go of her neck. She senses that you are afraid. Now, slowly push yourself back on the saddle and try not to spook her."

Don had done as he was told. He let go of the horse's neck and slowly pushed his body back and sat upright in his saddle. Some of his fear had left him as he sat for a moment while his horse remained calm and did not move.

As the cowboy rode away, he had turned in his saddle and yelled to Don, "Y'all might be fond of her, but she really would prefer a scoop of oats and a rub down when she's back in the barn."

Don had muttered to himself, "Oh yeah. You country yahoo. Y'all thinks you're real comedians."

The ranchers provided a huge Texas barbecue for their guests. Jim's three friends gorged themselves on beef brisket, Buffalo wings, pork ribs, and sausages—washed down with pitchers of beer. Being in the open air and out on the range all day, riding horses and pushing cows, gave Jim's buddies huge appetites. When they were finished with their excessive eating, they felt bloated and uncomfortable. They all were just really pleased to have gotten through the day in one piece.

# CHAPTER THIRTEEN

# LIFE PARTNERS

Judith Vennell met Jim Vincent at a wine tasting event in Napa, California. She was introduced to him by her eldest daughter, Janet, who was a member of the staff at the winery and was working that day as a server to the attendees.

Janet had met Jim several weeks before, when he had visited the winery to meet with the owner. She had enjoyed talking with him. When she saw him enter the wine tasting event, she thought that it would be a good opportunity for her to introduce him to her mother.

She had been looking for a man for her mother for some time. Her mother had been a widow for several years and she had been unsuccessful in finding anyone suitable. Her mother had also been reluctant to meet any new men.

Jim had been divorced twice and was not interested in developing a serious relationship.

On first impression, Judith appeared to him to be personable, bubbly, fun-loving, and a very nice person. He nicknamed her Peaches, and their friends soon began referring to her as Peaches.

Later, Jim learned that she was very conservative and managed her assets and her investments well. She had inherited a home with a vineyard and a stock portfolio from her parents. She had been able to significantly increase the value of both. She had had the help and support in investing from an old friend of her fathers, who had been his stockbroker for many years.

Jim and Peaches had been together as life partners for over thirty years.

Judith's best friend was Greta Mason. They had met when their two youngest children were in kindergarten. Greta had introduced herself to Judith one afternoon, showing up on her doorstep with both girls. Greta had picked up her daughter, Amy, from school and Amy insisted that her friend Karen come home with her. Greta took Karen to Karen's house and asked for Judith's permission to take the girls home with her to play. From then on, Judith and Greta have shared a friendship that has lasted over forty-five years.

Greta and her husband had moved from Napa fifteen years ago and lived two hours from Jim's ranch. Now, as a widow and eighty-two-years-old, she had experienced two falls. One inside her home and one outside in her garden. She had been trying to lift a granite stone in the garden when she fell and broke her hip. She had to be hospitalized for a few weeks, and it took more than six months for her to recover.

Peaches worried about Greta's health and safety. She would voice her concerns to Jim almost every day. Jim felt that he needed to come up with a solution.

While Greta was convalescing from her last fall, having broken her hip, Jim called and convinced her to list her home for rent in Lincoln and let her children manage it. He asked her to come to live in one of the guest houses on the ranch. She would be close to Judy. Jim's invitation to her was that she lives at the ranch for the rest of her days. Greta loved his proposal and said yes immediately! Jim could now keep an eye on both.

The Napa version of "Lucy and Ethel" would now be living close to one another and newly energized to launch new escapades.

Peaches and Greta were shopping fanatics. In the sports world, there are different levels of expertise. Many professional athletes fall into categories of Good, Great, or Elite during their careers. Very few are ever considered elite. Michael Jordan and Tom Brady have been considered elite in their respective sports.

Peaches and Greta were elite-level shoppers. Even though they each had a lot of cash in the bank, extensive stock portfolios, and personal property valued in the millions, they were addicted to the rush of the "Sale."

They watched the Quality Value Convenience (QVC) TV channel daily. They would call each other if one saw a special buy that would benefit the other. A few of their favorite QVC brand sellers were Susan Graver, Dennis Basso, Lori Goldstein, Cuddle Duds, and Beakman 1802 Skin & Body Care.

When they made plans to visit the outlet stores in Vacaville, their preparation was extensive. They wore very little make-up and brought their own shopping bags just in case a store wanted to charge them an extra $.10 for a bag.

When they arranged their gear for their shopping trips, they exchanged their larger purses for smaller ones. They wanted less bulk and an easier way to carry their money. They wore loose-fitting clothing, a small, thin top, and exercise pants. Running shoes were a must in order to maneuver easily between the store aisles.

Their preparations to attack the store sales reminded Jim of his own preparations for a night ambush in Vietnam.

It was 10 am on the tenth of October. The weather was unusually warm, a little hazy, and with no wind. It was considered an Indian Summer Day. Peaches and Greta had decided to take advantage of major sales opportunities in Napa stores. The Bel Aire Shopping Center was their first destination. They planned to visit Chicos, a woman's clothing store. They would move on to Whole Foods for produce and Target for water, paper plates, and toilet paper. They were in a hurry because they knew that many shoppers would be pursing the same sales items and they wanted to be there ahead of the crowd.

Peaches drove her car and Greta sat in the passenger seat of the Lexus SUV. As they approached the north end of the shopping center, they noticed that there were barricades (sawhorses) set up in the street.

When Peaches stopped her car, she and Greta looked at each other and Greta asked, "What do you think is going on?"

"It's probably one of those art exhibitions like they had here last week. We're not interested in that crap. We're here to shop. Get out and move that barricade. We're in a hurry," ordered Peaches.

When Greta got back into the car, Peaches drove forward into the mall and was stopped after traveling 200 feet. Two Napa policemen, in protective gear and carrying rifles, ran to the car and screamed at them to stop.

"Didn't you see the barricades? Get out of the car and get behind that dumpster. Now! We have a bank robbery in progress and you two are interfering with us," said one of the policemen.

The police were all over the shopping center. Sniper teams were stationed on the roofs of the buildings. Police units on the ground advanced cautiously towards the bank location.

Peaches and Greta huddled together, crouched down, behind a large blue garbage dumpster. They were there for over an hour before a policeman came and escorted them to their car. "Did you catch the robbers?" asked Greta.

"Lady, get in your car and get out of here," ordered a very annoyed officer.

The bank robbery had taken place at the south end of the Bel Air Shopping Center, next to a Mexican restaurant. The two masked robbers got away with two thousand dollars in cash. They disappeared into the shopping center and the Napa police were still looking for them.

When Peaches and Greta returned to the ranch house, Adele Garcia, the housekeeper, greeted them and said, "Senora, Jefe is very upset. He wants the two of you to meet with him in the living room. He is on a business call now and will meet with you when he finishes."

"Is something wrong?" asked Peaches.

"I don't know. I think it is something about the policia," replied Adele.

Peaches and Greta knew that Jim had learned what had transpired. If Jim knew that they had interfered with the police during the bank robbery, he would be very upset. They waited in the living room for him to finish his call. They were nervous and dreaded his reaction to their latest escapade.

Before he met with the two of them, Jim had consulted with Peaches' and Greta's six children. The children had immediately agreed with him that the two mothers should no longer be allowed to drive by themselves—ANYWHERE!

Source Delta had the responsibility of monitoring and protecting all members of Jim's family wherever they went. Following Peaches and Greta on their shopping trip to the Bel Aire Center, Source Delta observed the police ordering the two women out of their vehicle. They were to get behind a dumpster for protection. Source Delta immediately informed Jim that the police were pursuing a bank robbery at the south end of the shopping center. The police had directed Peaches and Greta to get behind a dumpster for protection.

When Jim finished his phone call, he went into the living room to confront Peaches and Greta. Before he had a chance to say anything, Peaches blurted out, "We didn't know it was a robbery. We thought it was one of those art exhibitions like they had there last week."

"Yea, we didn't see the cops. We didn't know there was a robbery going on," said Greta.

"You didn't recognize the police tape on the barricades? It didn't make you stop and think that something unusual was going on? You were too caught up in rushing to get to the sales. You didn't use common sense, and you became a problem for the police. They could have arrested the two of you for interfering with police operations," explained Jim.

"We're sorry Jim," whined Peaches. "We won't make that mistake again."

"You're right. You won't make that mistake again, because the two of you are done driving. I'm going to hire security for you, and they'll do the driving. I already spoke with the children and they agree with my decision. Your children agree with me too, Greta. You must understand that there are people out there who want to harm me, and anyone associated with me. We can't take chances and we must be alert when we are off the ranch. I'm not going to limit your travels at all. You will have security with you, and you must obey their orders. Is that clear?" asked Jim.

"You mean we can't drive anywhere? Even to the local grocery stores, or my friends' houses for bridge?" asked Peaches.

"You got it," said Jim. "Nowhere!"

Jim called Redline Group Security's Chairman, Victor Lewkowitz. Jim requested that Victor assign two female agents to the ranch. They were to provide protection for Peaches and Greta whenever they left the ranch for shopping or appointments. Two weeks later, Agents Jill Harris and Jolyn Nicol arrived and introduced themselves to Jim. He provided them with background on Peaches and Greta and explained why they needed special protection.

Jill Harris was 5'3" with a cute, freckled face and short hair. She had spent five years in the Army as a member of the Military Police (MP). She was an expert with handguns and rifles. She had survived two tours of duty in Afghanistan and was assigned duty as security of the Green Village compound that housed foreigners working for international service contractors. The compound came under attack and a huge explosion rocked the outer perimeter of the compound. Fortunately, there were no casualties during the attack. After leaving the Army, Harris applied to Redline Security Group and was quickly hired.

Jolyn Nicol was tall at 5'10" with blond hair and an attractive face. She projected a calm demeanor. She had spent five years in the Army and was also an expert marksman with handguns and rifles. She was assigned to the same unit in Afghanistan as Jill Harris, and they soon became good friends. When Harris was hired by Redline, she told the management that her good friend, Jolyn Nicol, was interested in joining them. Nicol was also soon hired by Redline.

Jim explained to the two security guards that they were to provide security for Peaches and Greta whenever they left the ranch. He was concerned that when they went into a dressing room while shopping or needed to use the restroom that they could be at risk. His requirement was that the two agents follow Peaches and Greta wherever they went. He explained that guarding them would not be an easy assignment.

"The two of them are strong-willed and they won't be happy having the two of you monitoring their every move. They won't like taking orders, but you must be firm with them and insist that they follow your directions. You will have my full support if they give you any crap. If they don't cooperate, you are to drive them home immediately," he said.

"We understand. We will create written guidelines for the two ladies and provide you, and them, with copies," replied Harris.

"That sounds great. I trust your judgement. You might find that your combat service in Afghanistan was easier than protecting these two!" Jim said.

Harris and Nicol laughed at Jim's remarks, and Nicol replied, "Thank you, sir. We appreciate your confidence in us."

# CHAPTER FOURTEEN

# THE FEDS WANT DETAILS

Jim received a call from FBI Assistant Director Arlene Gavon. She left a message asking for an appointment to meet with him at the ranch.

Director Gavon was one of only a few government employees that Jim liked and respected. She had visited him in the past with a group of government executives and had always conducted herself professionally. He respected her opinion and would listen to any proposals that she had to make.

The FBI had recently been involved in many scandals. Some of their employees were accused of mistreating American citizens. Top FBI executives had been forced to resign and were "walked out" of the FBI offices in disgrace. The leadership of the FBI had lost the respect and trust of many Americans.

When he returned Gavon's call, she informed him that a contingent of government employees from the FBI, Homeland Security, and the Department of Drug Enforcement (DEA) wanted to visit with Jim and the Source. They wanted to discuss the attacks on the drug cartels' processing plants and cash storage areas.

After the phone conversation with Director Gavon, Jim called his attorney and long-time friend, John Zuckero. John was a prominent attorney, now retired, but available to Jim for consultation. Years ago, Zuckero had represented Jim and his company in a lawsuit. They won a multi-million-dollar award from the court.

"John, I'm going to have another group of government visitors at the ranch to discuss the attacks on the drug cartels by the Source and me. Will you be available to sit in on our meeting next Thursday?" asked Jim.

"Definitely. I've been bored sitting around the house watching political programs and Netflix movies. What time do you want me to show up?" asked John.

"Well, they're supposed to be here by 11 am on Thursday. You're only ten minutes away. Drop-in about that time," said Vincent.

"Great. See you then. Oh, by the way, I recommend that you include your Palo Alto attorneys in the meeting with the government agencies. If something comes up in the discussions that might be a liability for you, it would be good to have your attorneys present. You can't trust anyone from the government agencies anymore," said John.

Vincent contacted Source Alpha and asked for a meeting to prepare for the visit of the government agencies.

"I plan to use the presentations that we used in our meetings to study and strategize for the attacks on the cartels. I'm also going to give them a little tutorial on how their agencies have failed, miserably, in their efforts to protect the American people," said Jim.

"When do you want to meet to prepare for our meeting?" asked Source Alpha.

"Let's start tomorrow morning at 8 am. It should take us four or five hours to go over all the information," said Jim.

"Source Bravo and I will be ready at that time," said Source Alpha.

In preparation for his strategy meeting with Source Alpha, Jim reviewed his extensive personal library of research topics. He had made copies of his data on the FBI, Homeland Security, and the DEA. He was especially interested in their budgets and personnel count. After all, these agencies were responsible for the protection of the American public. How were they spending their budget money and how were they staffing their personnel to address the most serious and immediate threats to the United States?

At 8 am the next morning, Jim, Source Alpha, and Source Bravo came together, by computer, to discuss his background information on the agencies. They spent five hours reviewing details on each of the agencies and their missions.

"I feel comfortable that we're ready for the meeting with the government agencies. I'm not familiar with any of the visitors except Director Gavon. Hopefully, they are sending us competent people and decision-makers to discuss the issues. I really hope that it won't be a waste of our time," said Jim.

After the meeting with Source Alpha and Bravo, and on John Zuckero's recommendation, Jim called the legal firm of Brushoff, Eddy, and Steffen, LLP, in Palo Alto, California. One of the lead attorneys in the firm, Patty Davis, had represented Jim when he had been subpoenaed to appear before the House Judiciary Committee in Washington, D.C.

When he reached Patty Davis, he explained that he wanted her to attend another meeting with government officials, but this time at his ranch.

Patty agreed to come to the meeting, and told him that she would ask her associate, and former college roommate, Carolyn Baggily, to attend the meeting.

Patty asked Jim, "Do you know all the members of this government group who are coming to meet with you? You should know by now, as well as anyone, that you can no longer trust any of the government agencies. Not that you really could have trusted them in the past, but they are acting extremely arrogant and unprofessional towards conservatives these days."

"I agree, Patty. I don't trust any of them. The FBI is poorly managed and corrupt at the top. The other agencies are stocked with left-wing activists who are looking for any opportunity to punish conservatives. We will not take them lightly. I'll want you to be there to look out for any 'landmines' they might try to plant for me," said Jim.

"No problem. We'll protect you against any nefarious attempts by the officials to take advantage of you, Jim," replied Patty.

"You might want to come to Napa the day before the meeting. You and your associate can stay in one of our cottages. We can meet and prepare for the meeting," said Jim.

"Thanks Jim. That's very generous of you. Carolyn and I will take you up on your offer. It will be easier for all of us to get organized for the meeting. See you at the ranch," said Patty.

<h1 style="text-align:center">CHAPTER FIFTEEN</h1>

# A VISIT FROM THE FEDS

On Thursday morning at 10:45, four vans pulled into the parking area of the ranch.

Director Gavon exited the first vehicle and positioned herself in order to introduce the other government visitors as they exited their vehicles.

John Zuckero had arrived at the ranch at 10:00 so that he and Jim would have plenty of time to prepare for the visitors. They were joined by Jim's Palo Alto attorneys, Patty Davis and Carolyn Baggily.

"Good morning, Jim. It's great to see you and Mr. Zuckero again," greeted Director Gavon.

"It's nice to see you too, Arlene. You're my favorite Fed. Please meet my attorneys, Patty Davis and Carolyn Baggily."

"I remember Patty from watching your testimony in Washington," said Gavon.

"Please introduce us to your companions," said Jim.

"Mr. James Vincent, please let me introduce Jared Collingsworth, Assistant Commissioner, Office Intelligence of the Customs and Border Protection.

"Anne Melloni, Deputy Administrator of the Drug Enforcement Administration, and their staff members.

"You might remember Agents Volpa and Neihaus from my office," said Director Gavon.

Altogether, there were three directors, six staff members, and four government security officers.

"Let's move onto the basketball court, where I have a conference table set up for your visit. You probably remember it from last time, Arlene. As a reminder, our meeting will be recorded and filmed, just as it was during our last meetings with government personnel.

"We have coffee, water, and soft drinks for you. At 1 pm, my cook will serve everyone a light lunch. Today it will be Mexican food," said Vincent.

"Are you in agreement for our meeting to be recorded and filmed?" Deputy Administrator Melloni asked Director Gavon.

"Yes, that is the procedure that we had agreed to the last time we met, Anne. Mr. Vincent will not meet with us unless he is able to record the meetings," said Director Gavon.

"Why is that Mr. Vincent? Is it really necessary to record our first meeting?" asked Deputy Melloni.

"Yes. Except for Director Gavon, I don't trust any government employees. The higher their rank, the less trust I have in them. There have been too many abuses to average Americans by government officials. My filming and recording of these meetings provide me with a certain level of confidence that my visitors will play it straight," said Vincent.

"Okay, sir. It's just that it is unusual for me to have meetings that are recorded in this manner," said Deputy Melloni.

"Suit yourself. No one is forcing you to have this meeting," said Vincent.

"You all may call me Jim. Hopefully, you have your drinks and are ready to begin. Before we field any questions from you about our attack on the cartels and their cash, the Source and I have prepared a presentation to address the concerns that we have," said Vincent.

Jim began his PowerPoint presentation. It was projected onto the large white screen in front of the conference table. He also had handouts of the presentation for each of the participants.

"Let me start with an overview, from our perspective, of each of the government agencies that you represent. I will begin by looking at the mission statements or priorities of each of your agencies:

## FBI

The FBI has approximately 35,000 employees, including special agents and support professionals.

The FBI budget for fiscal year 2021 was approximately $9.7 billion.

The FBI's stated mission is to, "Protect the American people and uphold the Constitution of the United States."

The FBI's stated priorities are to:

- Protect the U.S. from terrorist attack
- Protect the U.S. against foreign intelligence, espionage, and cyber operations
- Combat significant cyber-criminal activity
- Combat public corruption at all levels
- Protect civil rights

- Combat transnational criminal enterprises
- Combat significant white-collar crime
- Combat significant violent crime

## DEA

The DEA has over 10,000 employees, including 5,000 Special Agents and 800 Intelligence Agents.

The annual budget for the DEA is over $3 billion.

The DEA's Mission Statement is "To enforce the controlled substances laws and regulations of the United States and bring to the criminal and civil justice system of the United States, or any other competent jurisdiction, those organizations and principal members of organizations, involved in the growing manufacture or distribution of controlled substances appearing in or destined for illicit traffic in the United States and to recommend and support non-enforcement programs aimed at reducing the availability of illicit controlled substances on the domestic and international markets."

## HOMELAND SECURITY'S BORDER PATROL

The United States Border Patrol has over 20,000 agents.

The Border Patrol has an annual budget of over $3.9 billion.

(The annual budget of Homeland Security is over $1 trillion—Homeland Security would have significant additional monies to increase the Border Patrols budget, if necessary.)

The Border Patrol Mission is, "Securing U.S. borders between ports of entry...to detect and prevent the illegal entry of individuals into the United States...Together with other law enforcement officers, the Border Patrol helps maintain borders that work, facilitating the flow of legal immigration and goods while preventing the illegal trafficking of people and contraband."

"Ladies and gentlemen," Jim said, "your respective agencies have thousands of employees and hundreds of millions of dollars budgeted to operate your departments. Each of your agencies has the same mission to **'Protect the American people and uphold the Constitution of the United States.'**

"All of you have been doing a piss-poor job, and you have failed the American people.

"We have millions of immigrants invading our country and over 600,000 'got-aways.' To put these numbers in perspective, the state of Wyoming has approximately 580,000 citizens! No one knows where, in the United States, these illegals have gone! No one has any idea if some of these 'got-aways' may be terrorists who are planning to do harm to our citizens.

"We have opioids, specifically deadly fentanyl, being shipped over the border every day. Last year alone, over 100,000 Americans died from fentanyl poisoning. Some of the fentanyl has even been disguised as colored candy. Teenagers are consuming the drug and dying from it, almost immediately after intake."

**On October 19, 2022, ABC7 Eyewitness News reported that authorities seized 12,000 fentanyl pills at the Los Angeles Airport. The fentanyl was disguised in candy wrappers of Skittles, Whoppers, and SweeTarts.**

"A mother of a deceased child, poisoned by fentanyl, has recently described the current death toll from fentanyl as the equivalent of 'a plane crash a day, of people dying from fentanyl poisoning.'

"Your agencies don't need to wait for your headquarters in Washington D.C. to give you the okay to protect the American people. It's written in your mission statements. If you had been working together, you'd have more than sufficient resources to close the border from illegal entry and stop the drug trafficking.

"The death toll from fentanyl, in the last two years, is greater in number than the total of deaths from the Vietnam War, the two Gulf Wars, and the 20-year, Afghanistan War combined.

"Your agencies have got to get their asses down to the southern border and stop this catastrophe—immediately. You can justify taking these actions by pointing out that your agency mission statements, require you to do so.

"The FBI must stop their practice of raiding peoples' homes and putting elderly men in shackles. They should spend their resources ongoing after leaders of the drug cartels who are directly responsible for killing thousands of Americans.

"Maybe your departments consider the cartel leaders to be too dangerous for the FBI and DEA to pursue? After all, the cartels are well-known for beating, raping, butchering, and beheading their enemies. They have the Mexican government cowed and under their control. They operate without impunity in Mexico and Central America," said Jim.

"That's insulting," replied Deputy DEA Administrator Melloni. "Our agents are brave, and they will take on any enemy."

Jim continued, "It's not the field agents of the FBI and DEA that I have a problem with. I never question their bravery and I know that they do their duty, but they don't have any decision-making authority.

"As in the military, American troops on the ground fight very well and defeat the enemy every time. On the other hand, the military leaders in Washington D.C. continue to fail our troops in the field. Washington D.C. is controlled by politics—it is a swamp where patriotism goes to die.

"It's been this way, in every war since the Revolutionary War. If you know your history, you'll remember how General George Washington was always begging and fighting with Congress to get help and supplies for his Army. His Army went, for an entire winter, without shoes or enough food. Many of them starved!

"The same goes for the FBI and the DEA. The leaders in Washington are so caught up in partisan politics that they have forgotten their role and responsibility to the American people, and the commitment that they have made to support and follow the tenets of the Constitution."

"We'll take your presentation back to Washington and discuss it with our agencies. It's still not clear to me how we will be able to work with you. It seems that you have your own agenda. Are you willing to collaborate with our agencies?" asked Commissioner Collingsworth.

"It depends on how serious your agencies will be in respecting the data that we have provided to you. We've been very forthcoming with how we see the priorities. Hopefully, I have made it clear to you that we believe that you have failed in performing your agency missions. Let me know how and when you are willing to collaborate with us. We can get started immediately. We don't know if you want to be informed about our progress. You make the next move. We will continue to pursue our plans while we wait for your response," said Jim.

"I find you to be very arrogant, Mr. Vincent. You are taking it upon yourself to attack foreign nationals and their operations with not any communication with federal authorities. You are a rogue-player, and you must stop what you are doing," said Administrator Melloni.

# A CHANGING OF THE GUARD

The Democratic Party National Committee had to work quickly to fill the Vice-President vacancy.

They had finally decided on a replacement. The Vice-President had taken the oath of office of the President. The previous president, suffering from advanced Alzheimer's disease, had resigned. The newly sworn-in president pledged to her associates that she would only serve the last six months of her predecessors' term—until the next Presidential Election.

The Committee decided on Peter P. Assman as their choice for vice president. He was a Congressman from Illinois.

Assman was diminutive in stature. He was 5'3" and had a slim build. He had a record in congress of poor attendance and accomplishing almost nothing. He had voted 'present' more times than Obama had when Obama was Senator from Illinois. He was gay, outspoken, and articulate. That was an acceptable profile for the National Committee to choose him to fill the position.

Assman's parents were college professors. Both had declared that they were Marxists. Assman was an only child and was educated in the Marxist philosophy. He spent his college summers in Moscow and later lived in Havana for three months. When he married his husband, Charlie Gluman, they spent their honeymoon in Moscow.

His political opponents had described him as a cross between Alfred E. Neuman and Michael Dukakis. He always seemed to have a smirk on his face, and he had a habit of looking away or down while speaking. It was reminiscent of the mannerisms of Dukakis.

Whenever a reporter asked a challenging question, Assman typically would avoid it by purposely rambling on about issues that he favored. He would also bring up subjects that he preferred to discuss, such as climate change and electric cars. He was known for avoiding a reporter's original question, and other subjects that he felt were too challenging for him to answer.

Assman had always lacked a serious work ethic. He typically rode his bike to his office and arrived late most mornings. He would stay at the office for a few hours and then leave for home. He preferred to give speeches about what should be done. He never focused on fulfilling his commitment to the promises that he had made during his political campaign.

Assman publicly supported the indefensible crisis created by the Democratic Administration, that invited immigrants from all parts of the world to ignore American law and invade the southern border. This policy had resulted in immigrants experiencing horrifying levels of torture, sexual assault, child abuse, and death.

The Democratic National Committee had chosen a very weak and incompetent politician to assume the office of the vice president of the United States. He joined a very weak, and incompetent, president and they were the top leaders of the executive branch of government.

Assman's swearing-in ceremony recorded the second time in history that an unelected president and an unelected vice president headed the federal government's executive branch.

**On December 19, 1974, Nelson Rockefeller was sworn in as the forty-first Vice President of the United States. He had been nominated for the post by President Gerald Ford. The swearing-in ceremony highlighted the fact that it was the first time in history that both an unelected president and an unelected vice president headed the federal government's executive branch.**

## CHAPTER SEVENTEEN

# RETALIATION

Carlos Salinas knew that he didn't have much time left before the leaders of the cartels gave the order to eliminate him. They held him responsible for the loss of their cash and drugs. They had been demanding that he fix the problem. If he could not come up with an immediate solution, he was a dead man.

Salina's office in Los Angeles had completed a background check on Arturo Hernandez, the owner of the company hired by Jim to harvest his grapes. Now was the time to approach Arturo Hernandez and force him to hire hitmen to work among the grape harvesters on Jim's ranch.

Alex Arguello and Hector Diaz from Salinas' law firm in L.A., visited Arturo Hernandez at his office in Vallejo. After the initial exchange of greetings, Arguello got right to the point.

"Arturo. We would like you to hire a couple of our friends. They are new to the area, and they need a job. They will work hard and they will never be a problem for you," said Arguello.

"I am not looking to hire any new employees. Most of the people on my crews have been working for me for years and are dependable," said Hernandez.

"We understand. A powerful man in Mexico City would like you to hire our friends. You would be doing him a favor and he would be very grateful," said Diaz.

"Again, I don't need any more employees and I don't hire people that I don't know," said Hernandez.

"Okay. I'm going to make it more clear to you," said Arguello.

"This man in Mexico City is aware that your family is from Morelia. You are the oldest of four sons and three daughters. Your family immigrated to the United States in 1989. You still have aunts and uncles living in Morelia. Your wife, Marta, is from Jalisco and you live in Napa with your three daughters. Your parents are still alive. They live in Redwood City, but their health is not so good."

"What are trying to tell me—talking about my family history? Who's this man in Mexico City?" demanded Arturo.

"It's not important who he is. I'm telling you that the man wants you to do him a favor. If you refuse, you could be putting your family in danger. If you agree, the man will be indebted to you and will reward you. He will protect your family. Think about it. I'll call you tomorrow for your answer," said Arguello.

After the two men left his office, Arturo sat in his chair. He was stunned and frightened. It was very clear to him that this was a serious threat, and he would have to agree to hire the people. He knew it had to do with drugs. He didn't understand why they needed him to hire the men. He would never know. He guessed that they wanted their people embedded in the United States as part of their drug network.

Arguello called Arturo the next day for his answer. "I'll hire your guys, but they must be capable of work. I can't have them sitting on their asses collecting a check," said Arturo.

"Good decision. The man in Mexico will be pleased. Don't worry. They will be your hardest workers. It should be clear to you that you can't mention our conversation to anyone. Not even your wife," said Arguello.

"It's clear to me. No one will know," replied Arturo.

# CHAPTER EIGHTEEN

# HARVEST TIME

Carlos Salinas was living on borrowed time. The leaders of the cartels had threatened to kill him. Carlos promised them that he would take care of the old man in Napa, who they believed was responsible for their losses.

Salinas had explained to them that the old man was well-guarded, 24-hrs a day, but that he had a plan to overcome the security at the ranch. He promised one of the cartel leaders that he would eliminate the old man before the "Day of the Dead."

The cartel leader replied, "That better be the case, or you will join your ancestors!"

The "Day of the Dead" or "Dia de los Muertos," is a holiday traditionally celebrated on November first or second, depending on the locality. It is widely observed in Mexico and is also observed in other locations by people of Mexican heritage. It is a holiday of joyful celebration. The multi-day holiday involves family and friends who gather to pay their respects. They remember friends and family members who have died. Many celebrants build home altars called "ofrendas" and have favorite foods and beverages of the departed.

Salinas' plan to kill Jim involved taking advantage of the timing of the grape harvesting in the Napa Valley.

Each year from late July and into November, the Napa Valley comes alive with the excitement of harvesting grapes. The grapevines are tended to year-round. Once the grapes reach their peak ripeness, the workers race to complete the harvesting. The grapes are harvested when their sugar levels or 'Brix' match the required level.

Varietals of grapes are harvested at different times during the grape harvesting months.

Grapes for sparkling wines are usually the first to be picked. That happens around the end of July or the beginning of August. They are followed by Sauvignon Blanc, Chardonnay, Pinot Noir and early reds like Merlot, Zinfandel and Syrah.

Harvesting of Cabernet Sauvignon grapes, in the Napa Valley, begins later than most varietals.

It was 6 am on the twentieth of October. Arturo Hernandez's grape harvesting crew arrived to harvest the Cabernet vineyard on Jim's ranch.

Embedded among Hernandez's crew were Javier Romero and Pepe Cortez. Hernandez had agreed to hire them, due to pressure put on him with the threat to his family. They were hired killers from Pico Rivera in southeastern Los Angeles, County. Pico Rivera is a small city situated eleven miles from downtown Los Angeles.

Both killers had prison records. They had served time for minor offenses. They had attended Junior College and were better educated than the gang members in their neighborhood. They had recently participated in two, for hire, killings. They eliminated a local gang leader and his lieutenant.

They had been hired to kill Jim and anyone living on the ranch.

At the 10 am break time, Romero and Cortez walked away from the break area and moved cautiously towards the ranch house. Each carried a pistol with a suppressor. Their weapons were wrapped in a t-shirt. As they approached the back door, Security Guard Jill Harris, came around the west-side of the building and took a firing stance. The killers were surprised by her and raised their pistols to shoot. Harris shot Romero in the chest and he went down. Cortez immediately ducked behind a bush but was shot twice in the back by another security guard, Jolyn Nicol, who came from the east-end of the house.

Romero was dead, having been shot through the heart. Cortez was badly wounded but would live.

The Redline Group had assigned Harris and Nicol to the ranch as personal bodyguards for Peaches and Greta. They had not uttered a word before bringing down the two killers. After confirming that the killers had been neutralized, Harris calmly radioed the command center and requested an ambulance to remove Cortez.

Four days after the shootings, Victor Lewkowitz, Chairman of the Redline Security Group, arrived at the ranch. He was accompanied by three of his employees. He asked to meet with Jim.

When they met in Jim's office, Lewkowitz explained,

"Mr. Vincent. As you may know, when one of our employees is involved in a shooting, they must take a two-week leave of absence. We then assign them to new duties in a different location."

"No. I wasn't aware of your policy, Victor, but I understand why you would have one. We were very pleased with the work Harris and Nicol did as security guards for Peaches and Greta. We feel fortunate that they were here to intercept the killers," said Jim.

"We are very proud of them, too. Now, I'd like to introduce you to their replacements. Mr. Vincent, please meet Security Agents Susan Stubbs and Heather Strong. They are very experienced in personal protection. We are confident that they will perform their duties as well as Harris and Nicol did," said Lewkowitz.

"I'm very pleased to meet the two of you. Allow me to provide you with a brief summary of Peaches and Greta. You will need to understand what a challenging mission you have agreed to undertake," said Jim.

On November second, the "Day of the Dead", Carlos Salinas was assassinated in his office, in Mexico City, by two gunmen. He had been shot nine times.

## CHAPTER NINETEEN

# A ROGUE MISSION

FBI Agent Peter S. Paul met with Assistant Director of the FBI, Beth Booksin, in her office at FBI headquarters. She had summoned Paul to her office for a private meeting. Booksin had been impressed with Paul's capabilities. They had worked together on a Russian counterespionage mission in 2018.

"Good morning, Peter. How are Melissa and the children?" asked Booksin.

"We're all fine Director. How's your family?" Paul replied.

Booksin's fondness for Paul was not reciprocated. Paul was disgusted by homosexuals. He was very much aware that Booksin was a lesbian, and that she had a female lover who worked at the Justice Department.

Booksin felt confident that her relationship was a secret, but she was seriously mistaken and naïve. She was jeopardizing her career, even though government policy accepted lesbian relationships. FBI internal monitors knew of her liaison with a new lover shortly after their first meeting at a local gay bar. They also knew that they were sleeping together.

"Peter, I want to discuss something very confidential. This meeting is off the record," said Booksin.

"Okay. I'm all ears and as far as our conversation is concerned, it never happened," said Paul.

"Thank you, Peter. As you are aware, Deputy Gavon is very fond of that old veteran in California who has been stirring things up—Jim Vincent. I believe Vincent is a threat to this country and has been operating aggressively, unchecked, by any law enforcement agencies. This can't continue. He needs to be stopped—now! I want him investigated and arrested. If you're in agreement with me, I'd like you to head up a team and go out to California and bring him in," said Booksin.

"Are you sure you want to take such extreme measures, Director Booksin? Our actions could create a backlash that could fall on you personally. Vincent has become a hero to many on the right," said Paul.

"I'm not afraid of any backlash. We have convincing evidence that Vincent has violated federal law. We must reign him in and force him to be accountable," said Booksin.

"I'm interested in taking on the mission if it's officially sanctioned by the Administration," said Paul.

"Don't worry. I'll have all the necessary signatures, including the Director's, to go forward with the mission. Just get ready to choose your team and move on the project. And keep it quiet," said Booksin.

"Yes ma'am. I'll get on it immediately," said Paul.

It was 6:30 am when Jim Vincent was alerted by Source Delta that a convoy of four vehicles had entered the road that led to the ranch. Source Delta was able to identify that most of the occupants in the vehicles were wearing baseball caps, jackets, and flak vests. The vests were stenciled with the letters FBI.

"This is strange," Jim remarked to Source Delta. "I would have thought that Director Gavon would have contacted me if there was going to be a meeting with the FBI. Please be ready to act against these people if they have come here with bad intentions."

"We are ready. Let us know what action you want us to take," said Source Delta.

"They are not going to remove me from my ranch without my permission. Please stop them if it becomes necessary. Just don't kill any of them," said Jim.

Jim stood in his entryway with a cup of coffee in his right hand and a cell phone in his left. One of his security personnel, Susan Stubbs, stood behind him. When the convoy rolled into the ranch driveway, Jim stepped forward to greet the occupants as they exited the vans.

Eight FBI agents carrying rifles surrounded Jim as he stood drinking his coffee.

"Did you fellas get lost? There's no deer hunting in these parts of the Napa Valley," said Jim.

"Very funny, Mr. Vincent. We are here to arrest you and take you back to Washington, D.C. Allow me to read you your rights," announced Special Agent Peter Paul.

"I know my rights and you're not taking me anywhere," said Jim.

"Come on now, Mr. Vincent. Cooperate and no one will be harmed. Turn around so Agent Thomas can handcuff you," said Paul.

"Don't try to cuff me, son," said Jim to Agent Jim Thomas. "Let's just stand back and look at the vehicle that you want to use to take me away."

Instantaneously, the van Jim had pointed to exploded. Its four tires and windows disintegrated. The van's idling engine shut down as the wiring throughout the vehicle was completely fried.

Everyone except Jim was stunned. Before anyone could say anything, the other three vehicles also exploded.

Two of the FBI Agents fell to the ground. They soon realized their rifle barrels were bent and looked as if they had melted. The agents were shocked and frightened.

Agent Paul was stunned by the four explosions. He was, at first, speechless, but as he regained his composure, he began shouting.

"You're leaving with us, Mr. Vincent. Even if we have to walk all the way to Napa."

"That's not going to happen. If one of your agents takes a step towards me, you will pay the price, Agent Paul," said Jim.

"Agent Thomas. Cuff the son-of-a-bitch, now," ordered Paul.

Agent Thomas hesitated, not moving. Paul grabbed the cuffs out of Thomas's hand and began to move towards Jim.

As Paul took his second step, he screamed in pain. A laser-like light burned through his right shoe, destroying his toes, and leaving him missing half of his foot. The intense heat from the laser immediately cauterized the wound, so there was little bleeding. Paul rolled around on the ground, screaming, as fellow agents came running to his aid, trying to stop him from moving.

Jim immediately went into action and yelled to Agent Stubbs to call Queen of the Valley Hospital in Napa. Stubbs immediately called for a helicopter. The helicopter at the Queen was used to fly wounded from automobile and other accidents to the hospital. It had been especially busy when the Napa Valley had suffered severe fires. Many people had been injured and had to be rescued.

Within half an hour of the call for help, the helicopter landed at the ranch to fly Paul to the hospital.

"You're going to pay for this, Vincent. We're going to get you good, you son of a bitch," cried Paul as he lay on the stretcher, waiting to be loaded into the helicopter.

"The time has come for you bastards to be held accountable for your Gestapo-style tactics. You've been abusing American citizens and getting away with it. That stops now. You're one of the first to suffer the consequences, Agent Paul, but you won't be the last. Now, get the hell off my property and never return, asshole," yelled Jim.

After the helicopter had left the ranch carrying Special Agent Paul, the remaining FBI agents began to walk the three miles from the ranch to the

Silverado Country Club parking lot. They had called ahead for FBI personnel to pick them up. Jim called two towing companies in Napa and asked them to send their tow trucks to remove the four destroyed FBI vans from his property.

When all visitors had left, Jim spoke to Source Delta. "Let's execute our plan against their headquarters."

"We will do it now," responded Source Delta.

The following day, at two in the morning, east coast time, FBI headquarters lost power on all floors of the building. The wiring throughout the building had been destroyed and the office equipment became unusable. All computer files in the offices on each floor were deleted.

Later that morning, many high-level FBI personnel found it impossible to drive to work. The wiring in their government vehicles had been destroyed. They had to resort to driving their personal vehicles if they wanted to go anywhere. The Director's driver had to use his own car to pick up the Director at his home. The Director would soon learn that he didn't have an office to go to.

The Department of Justice (DOJ) launched an investigation into the FBI's raid on Jim's ranch. The investigators soon learned that Assistant Director Booksin had not sought, nor received, clearance from her superiors to pursue the arrest of Jim Vincent.

Assistant Director Booksin was forced to resign. She was scheduled to attend a hearing in two days. The hearing would determine her future and the disposition of her pension.

# CHAPTER TWENTY

# ROOTING OUT EVIL

Jim and the Source targeted certain city and state governments to be punished. They chose governments that had encouraged and supported the uncontrolled crime wave sweeping the country. As their first targets, they chose three cities and states with the highest crime and murder rate.

They believed the best way to root out evil was to immobilize state and local governments and render them inoperable. They decided that if the leaders of these governments were not going to uphold the law, then they would make sure that the governments would not be able to function at all. If a government could not function, it could not do harm to the people. The only exception to their policy would be to maintain the functions and operations of all police departments.

Jim and the Source began with the state of Illinois and the city of Chicago.

While the morbidly obese governor of Illinois was eating his breakfast, he received a call on his home phone from his driver. The driver informed him that his limousine had broken down.

"What's wrong with the car?" bellowed the Governor.

"It's dead sir. It's not just the battery. The wiring throughout the car has been 'fried.' I've never seen anything like this. If it is all right with you, can I pick you up in my car?" asked the driver.

"That's a good idea. When will you be able to get here?" asked the Governor.

"I can be there in forty-five minutes, sir. I hope you don't mind riding in an old Toyota," said the driver.

"I don't care. Just get me to my office," replied the Governor.

"Okay, sir. I'll be there in forty-five," said the driver as he hung up.

When the Governor and his driver arrived at the Governor's office, they noticed that there were about twenty people standing around the entrance to the building.

The Governor asked two members of his staff, "What's going on here?"

"The building has been closed down, sir. We tried to reach you on your cell phone," said a staff member.

"Yeah. My phone is dead. What the hell is going on?" he asked.

Later in the afternoon, the Governor returned to the Governor's mansion. He found it severely damaged and uninhabitable.

The mayor of Chicago was a woman who resembled the character Yoda from the Star Wars movie. She was dwarf-like at 4'10" and had bulging eyes and a high forehead. She hated white people, even though her wife and her two adopted children were white and hispanic. She would only accept interviews with minority reporters. Her staff members were in constant fear of her nasty disposition.

She had been a dedicated political hack in the Democratic Party for over twenty-years before being elected mayor. She had been very capable of using her minority ethnicity to her benefit. It allowed her to rise in the ranks of her party.

Chicago's City Hall is a ten-story building that was completed in 1911. It houses the official seat of the government of the City of Chicago. It is located at 121 N LaSalle Street. The building has the offices of the mayor, city clerk, and city treasurer. It also contains the offices of the Aldermen of Chicago's wards and chambers of the Chicago City Council.

At 2 am on Monday morning, the offices and equipment in Chicago's City Hall became inoperable. Office equipment was destroyed and computer systems on all floors were disabled. The wiring throughout the building was fried. There was no access to the internet and electronic files in all offices were destroyed. There was flooding throughout the building due to broken pipes. The windows on all floors had been blown out. Chicago's City Hall headquarters had been destroyed.

The mayor was forced to re-locate her offices to the headquarters of the Chicago Police Department at 3510 S. Michigan Ave. She was very upset and afraid due to her disabled office building. She believed the attack on City Hall was a direct attack on her. She was convinced that it was an attack by right-wing racists who hated her and her lifestyle.

Illinois was not the only state to receive attacks on their State and City government headquarters. New York's state government headquarters in Albany was attacked and the City Hall of New York City experienced extreme damage to its main building.

Washington D.C.'s city hall offices at 950 24th Street Northwest, was the third target for destruction by Jim and the Source.

**Washington D.C., formally the District of Columbia, is the capital city and federal district of the United States. The U.S. Constitution provides for a federal district under the exclusive jurisdiction of Congress. The Residence Act on July 16, 1790 approved the creation of the capital district located on the Potomac River. A locally elected mayor and a thirteen-member council have governed the district since 1973. Congress maintains supreme authority over the city and may overturn local laws. The city has a population of approximately 690,000 residents.**

**With a crime rate of sixty per thousand residents, Washington, D.C. has one of the highest crime rates in the United States. Based on FBI reported crime data, a person's possibility of becoming a victim of one of these crimes is one in one-hundred.**

Jim placed a call to his friend, Arlene Gavon, FBI Assistant Director. "Arlene. I wanted you to be one of the first to know why we have targeted the government buildings in Illinois, New York, and Washington D.C.," explained Jim.

"I'm aware of the attacks. Several people in my office rushed to tell me about the attacks shortly after they happened. You know, we must meet as soon as possible. Jim, they think that this is another one of your 'shit storms' and they are putting the blame on me. They are convinced that you and I are good friends, and they believe you probably forewarned me and I didn't report it," complained Gavon.

"Well, we are friends, aren't we? I've been telling everyone that you are the only Fed I trust," said Jim.

"I know, Jim, but where do we go from here? I've got to tell them something, or they might plan another raid at your home," said Gavon.

"The states and cities we chose are in chaos and out of control. The governors and mayors have ignored their fiduciary responsibilities to the people. We believe that if the governments are immobilized, they will do less harm to the people. They must support their police departments and take the cities back from the criminals," said Jim.

"Why have you targeted the governors?" asked Gavon.

"Because they could stop the crime waves if they wanted to and they're doing nothing. I think they believe that politically, it's in their best interest to do nothing. They don't care about the people. They are only concerned about maintaining their power," said Jim.

"What message do you want me to convey to the powers that be here?" asked Gavon.

"The FBI maintains extensive statistics on murder rates and the crime wave raging throughout the country. They don't need me to tell them how bad things are. They should send agents to all state governments and the largest city governments. They should inform them that they must take the control away from the criminals immediately. If they don't, the problems will escalate and get even worse," replied Jim.

# CHAPTER TWENTY-ONE

# A PAUSE IN TIME

Bill Andrew was visiting Jim at the ranch. It was early evening, and they were both relaxing and enjoying their favorite cocktails.

"Jim. You and the Source could rule the world. Why don't you?" asked Bill.

"It was never our intention to dominate anyone or any country. We just wanted to root out the evil that was threatening to do the most harm to mankind," replied Jim.

"You could have taken out many of those bad actors who were enslaving, abusing, and killing people. How about those Iranian Ayatollahs, Putin, Xi, or that fat, little North Korean? If you had taken them out, it would have saved a lot of lives and prevented a lot of misery," said Bill.

"Bill. You know as well as I do that those bastards would have been replaced by others before their bodies were cold. It's up to the people of those countries to 'rise up' and fight for their freedom—like we Americans did against the British.

"We learned a big lesson in Vietnam, Bill. When you fight for others and they don't, or won't, fight for themselves, they will eventually be defeated. Freedom is never free. You must earn it and you must be ready to fight to keep it," said Jim.

"I read a recent article about Generation X, you know, those between the ages of twenty-five and forty. The article said that only 35% of them considered themselves patriotic," said Bill.

"I'm not surprised to hear that data. There will be a reckoning for them in the future and it will not be pleasant. Americans need to feel pain and loss on almost every important issue before they will wake up and see the light. China is encroaching on every aspect of our lives, and when people finally wake up and realize it, it will probably be too late!" said Jim.

The following day, late in the afternoon, Jim was in his office on his computer discussing the next steps with the Source.

"Jim, what do you want to target next?" asked the Source.

"Climate change might be a consideration. You won't believe the scams that have been perpetrated against the people of the world by special interest groups. They are promoting the fear of climate change. Trillions of dollars that should have been spent for humanitarian purposes, have been wasted on corrupt programs attempting to resolve questionable climate change issues.

"Another target is China. China's global ambition to dominate the world is a great concern. They are bribing officials in many third-world countries for the purpose of taking control of their governments. They are harvesting and exploiting the natural resources of those countries and are exporting them to China for domestic consumption," replied Jim.

"Source. I've never seen you. I have only witnessed your capabilities. I would like to see what you look like," said Jim.

"It is not important for you to see me, Jim. You know who—
**I AM."**

# COMING SOON—A NEW NOVEL

## From JAMES PEIFER

# THE VIGILANTE

There are many "shadow governments" throughout the world. They consist of central banks, intelligence agencies, think tanks, globalist elites, and moneyed interests. These are the true power behind global governments. The official elected government is subservient to the shadow government, which is the real executive power.

James Greaney is one of the most powerful men in the world but is known only to a few.

He oversees a network of global corporations that are valued in the billions of dollars.

The few individuals who know him describe him as forward-thinking, cunning, wise, even-tempered, and amiable. He is feared and cruel at times. He wouldn't hesitate to use violence if he deemed it necessary.

He has identified the global shadow governments and they are his targets.

He has become "the shadow" behind the shadow governments.
**James Greaney is—The Vigilante!**

# About the Author

James Peifer is a retired business owner from Silicon Valley.
He was an Army Captain and a combat veteran of the Vietnam War.
He lives in Napa, California.